THE NAVAJO MASKS MYSTERY

A Chile Charlie Tale

By

GEORGE PINTAR

Second Edition August 2023

Design Cover by KDP

ISBN:9798859798445

ACKNOWLEDGMENTS

Thanks to my family, colleagues, and editors for encouraging me to write this book. Thanks to Bob Worthington, Maryann Costa, Janice Alexander, Efrem Carrasco, Austin, and Lindsey Jones for contributing thoughts, experiences, and research for this book. Each was helpful and supportive.

I want to thank my caregiver, Mary Holguin, who provided caregiving services while working on this book.

On a personal note, a huge thanks to my wife, Jean Natalie Pintar (Deceased), for bearing with me during the writing phase of this adventure. She always supported and encouraged me to write. Jean died before this book was published, but she would have approved this story.

TABLE OF CONTENTS

PROLOGUE

Jimmy Running Water and his childhood friend, Chris Leaping Bear, were of the Navajo Warm Springs Tribe near Gallup, New Mexico. It was early December. They sat under a fully grown Chinese elm tree and spoke with disgust of the poverty conditions of the reservation and the hardships they'd endured all their lives. They talked about what they wanted, primarily items of self-gratification like new clothes, money for entertainment, and a decent truck. Both Jimmy and Chris were twenty years of age and jobless. There weren't many good-paying jobs on the reservation that suited them, plus they lacked the skills and training for high-paying federal jobs. They were boys cast only for blue-collar jobs. Their only obstacle was laziness, and their only hope was crime.

Jimmy Running Water spent most of his teenage years engaged in misdemeanor crimes, mostly thefts from stores, unsuspecting tourists, family members, and, occasionally, livestock from local ranches. Chris Leaping Bear had always been Jimmy's lackey and complicit partner. Together, they had been arrested numerous times.

"Why did you ask me to meet you here," Leaping Bear asked Jimmy.

"I found a way to make enough money for us to get out of this godforsaken reservation," Running Water said.

"Like what? We can't go back into construction again. Everybody thinks we stole their tools. We're lucky they didn't call the cops."

Running Water gave Chris a dismissive wave of his hand. "Eh, don't worry about it. Trefren may be a Policeman, but he's my cousin, and you know what they say, 'Blood is thicker than whisky.'"

"Yeah, maybe, but I don't think he likes you. You better stick to the whisky."

Running Water smiled. "Greystone told me about a job and gave me the number of a man to call."

"Did you call him?"

"Yeah. The man told me about the black market for Indian relics and a storehouse full of valuable stuff at the Native American Museum in Gallup. He said there's a collection of Navajo Kachina Ceremonial

2

masks in the Inventory Room worth thousands of dollars," Jimmy said excitedly. "I want those masks.

The question is, how do we get them? Any ideas?"

"No, you're always the one with the ideas," Chris replied.

Running Water thought for a moment. "Okay then. I want you to go to the museum, check out the layout, especially where the back door is, and check out the security system. What is the night security guard's routine? Find out what times he checks the doors and how often. I wanna know everything."

"Okay. Sounds good to me."

"Meet me back here at one o'clock in three days. Then, we'll come up with a plan. I have other things I need to check out," Jimmy said.

The boys met again three days later under the same Chinese elm tree, which had lost half of its leaves by then.

"So, what did you find out?" Jimmy Running Water asked as he rubbed his hands to keep them warm.

"I discovered it would be hard to sneak into the museum. The security guard gets there at five p.m. and starts to make his rounds after all the employees leave. He checks all doors to ensure none have been left open by accident and rechecks them about every two hours during his entire shift. His desk is just inside and faces the front door," Leaping Bear reported. "I thought he might fall asleep, but the man stays awake all night. I don't think we can get in undetected."

"We'll have to figure something out, then," Jimmy said.

"You mean we're still going to try to steal those masks anyhow?"

Jimmy gave his friend a sinister grin. "Oh yes, we're going to get those masks for sure. It'll make a nice Christmas present."

Jimmy and Chris arrived at the front door of the Native American Museum at 8:15 p.m. that evening. They wore dark, hooded jackets and dirty, tattered clothes that made them look like vagrants, and each carried a small ceremonial drum. They sat with their backs to the front door and began beating their drums with a slow, rhythmic sound that could barely be heard inside the museum. As time passed, the drums became louder and louder until the security guard finally got up from his chair, unlocked the front door, and stepped outside.

"You boys get . . ."

Before the guard completed his warning, Jimmy Running Water sprung up and grabbed him from behind in a tight bear hug. The guard struggled but was helpless against the powerful grip of his assailant. Chris Leaping Bear took a bottle of ether from his coat pocket and soaked it in a white handkerchief. He placed it tightly over the guard's mouth and nostrils. Jimmy turned his head to avoid a whiff of the ether. The guard fell limp in Jimmy's muscular arms within a few seconds.

They dragged the security guard inside and tied him upright in his chair with his head slumped down. The boys found their way to the Inventory Room and searched all the shelves filled with Native American relics. They rummaged throughout the room and the shelves until they found four Kachina Ceremonial masks wrapped in red velvet cloths in a wooden case. From inside his jacket, Chris Leaping Bear pulled a large black cotton sack and carefully placed the box in it. All was quiet, and the guard did not stir. The boys left through the back door, which locked automatically behind them.

Two hours after the break-in, Running Water and Leaping Bear arrived at the base of a canyon far north of the city. It was four weeks until Christmas, and the temperature hovered nearly thirty-two degrees. They pulled the hoods of their jackets tightly against their faces to keep warm.

He had scouted the canyon a few days before and found a good spot to bury the sacred masks — between a large piñon juniper tree and the canyon wall. The desert looked different in the dark, but with flashlights and considerable time, they found the spot. "Get the shovels out of the truck, and let's hide our treasure," Jimmy ordered.

The digging began. Chris dug a four-foot square hole, four feet deep, while his friend held the flashlights. Jimmy placed the sack into the hole and carefully covered it with loose red earth to not pack it too tight.

"You think we'll be able to find this place two weeks from now," Chris asked.

"Yeah, I am sure I'll remember this place." He placed two large, red sandstone rocks on the covered hole to mark the spot. He stepped back and admired his work. "It's going to be a good Christmas," Jimmy said. The two boys celebrated with whiskey and danced to their truck's radio music.

Jimmy broke branches off a nearby tree and used them to smooth the ground over the freshly dug hole. They walked to their truck, dragging the bushes behind them to conceal their footprints on the loose sand, then tied them to the truck's bumper. They drove away, erasing any trace of their presence, and disappeared into the darkness.

◆◆◆◆◆◆◆◆◆◆

Dr. Lean Acothley, the Museum Director, arrived early the following morning and found his security guard bound to a chair. He called the Gallup Police Department immediately and inspected the entire museum for stolen items.

When the police arrived, the night security guard reported that he was overwhelmed by two vagrants wearing hooded jackets, and that was all he could remember. The police asked for a list of stolen items.

"Nothing of value has been taken," the Director replied.

Chapter One

The Journey

Chile Charlie was sound asleep when he felt movement on his mattress. Sir Gallagher, his seven-year-old furball cat, had found his way onto Charlie's chest. His six a.m. ritual told his master it was time to face the new day. Charlie's eyes were still closed as he gave Sir Gallagher his morning back and belly rub.

"Thanks, Gallagher, you're a good alarm clock," he said in a raspy voice.

Sir Gallagher had done his duty. He jumped from the bed and waited for Charlie to do the same. It was a struggle. It took another fifteen minutes before his feet finally touched the floor. He followed his buddy to the kitchen, opened a can of kitty food, and pushed the start button on the coffee maker.

Chile Charlie lived in a condo on the second floor of a small complex. It was a modest home. His front door faced the city of Las Cruces, New Mexico. It led to a sitting room with two hallways, each leading to separate bedrooms. The kitchen in the back was sufficiently large for a single man. The back door in the kitchen opened to a concrete landing with stairs to the parking lot. Next to the kitchen was the living room with a glass sliding door that provided a panoramic view of the Organ Mountains and opened to a private patio. It was a comfortable home but lonely. Charlie glanced out the rear sliding glass door to view the sunrise — another day.

He sat in the living room gazing at the mountains for almost an hour until the sun broke over the peaks. The sun shone brightly, with no clouds to clutter the view of the blue sky or morning fog to cover the majestic mountain peaks. God must have used his magical brush to paint this scene for me, Charlie thought, but it didn't bring a smile to his face, unlike before. Charlie hadn't smiled for some time. Gloom and sadness had set in his heart. He sat on his leather chair for another hour before he got up to dress for his daily jog. He moved with sluggish motions as if lacking purpose.

A dirt hiking trail was less than fifty yards from his back door, and every morning, come rain or shine, Charlie took his five-foot, eleven-inch frame for a two-mile run. He enjoyed running the picturesque narrow canyons and rocky arroyo trails and watching the desert's wildlife. Lately, it has been his only tranquility from his mental burdens.

The first mile started with a slow military jog, then a faster jog, and finally, a fast run for the last quarter of a mile. He returned an hour later. The final fifty yards of his run were slightly uphill, which gave his cardiovascular system a good workout. Although Chile Charlie was in good physical condition for a forty-eight-year-old man, he breathed heavily, exhausted from his run. He bent over and placed his hands on his knees to regain normal breathing, but he still had stairs to climb. Determinately, he ran up the stairs, two steps at a time, until he reached the top landing to the kitchen door.

Charlie stepped inside and slumped down onto a chair nearest the patio sliding door. Charlie hadn't caught his breath when he heard a banging at the kitchen door. It was his neighbor, Bob, who lived in the condo below. They had become friends when Charlie first moved in eighteen months ago. Bob was in his early forties and had a couch potato physique. He did not exercise much. Bob motioned that he wanted in, and Charlie reluctantly forced himself to get up and unlock the door.

"Why am I blessed with your presence this morning, Bob," Charlie asked.

"Wait, let me catch my breath first. Those stairs are killers. No matter how slowly I climb them, I always need time to regain my breath. I'm sure the 3,900-foot elevation has something to do with it," Bob said.

"Bob, you'd suffocate if you lived in Colorado. The elevation is a mile high there." Charlie gave Bob a grin as if to say, find a better excuse for being out of shape.

The tone in Charlie's voice did not go unnoticed. Bob helped himself to a glass of water and drank it in three large gulps. "I came up here to check on you, to see how you're doing. I noticed you haven't been yourself for some time now."

"Thanks, but I don't need any looking after."

"It's been quiet up here. My wife and I don't hear the Randy Granger, Carlos Nakai, or any other Native American music that you used to play all the time. We kind of like that music."

"The CDs are on top of the stereo. Take them if you miss them so much," Charlie said almost angrily.

"You never talked like that to me before, Charlie. This is not you. What's going on with you?"

Charlie realized he had hurt his friend's feelings. "I'm sorry, Bob. You're right. I'm just going through some things right now."

"What kind of things?"

"Nothing I care to discuss?"

"Nothing you care to discuss. Do you know whom you're talking to? I'm a psychologist, remember? And more than that, I'm your friend. I can help you work through whatever's weighing on your mind."

Charlie inhaled deeply, held the air briefly, and released it. "Too many things have gone wrong in my life, Bob—my divorce from my high school sweetheart after sixteen years of marriage. I lost my wife, four children, and home. It was my fault, though."

"You never told me about that, Charlie."

"It's too painful to talk about. But there's more to it. I later met this wonderful woman, and we were married for six years . . . she died three years ago. Cancer took her away from me," he said with quivering lips and downcast eyes. "I started drinking heavily and pretty much lost everything. I only had my tractor, so I moved here to escape all those memories."

"Wow. I didn't know that." Bob was disappointed that he didn't know his friend as well as he thought.

"It doesn't matter where you move," Charlie said, "the memories always follow you and sometimes haunt you. It hit me suddenly and has eaten at me for a long time."

"You know, Charlie, words can't fix a man. They can only direct him. And you can't go around searching for answers. Sometimes, the answers will find you. But you must have an open mind and an open heart."

Bob looked about the room. He saw the stack of Native American music on the entertainment shelf. "You know, there's a reason this place is called the Land of Enchantment, and there's a reason you ended up here. Maybe you should travel up north and find a priest from one of those old missions to guide you, or perhaps . . . some Indian shaman on the reservations."

The room was silent for a few minutes.

"You know, Bob, for a psychologist, you sure give strange advice, but maybe that's what I need.

Chapter Two

Land of Enchantment

Charlie spent most of the morning having his 1959 El Camino serviced for his journey. The afternoon was spent at the Mesilla Valley Mall buying new clothes and a giant suitcase to put them in. It was almost 4:00 p.m. when his car was packed and ready to go. Charlie placed his dark, earth-colored military backpack on the passenger seat. He stepped back to admire his car, a newly painted 1959 El Camino, a cream color with a turquoise stripe from front to back. The colors of the earth, he thought.

Charlie honked his horn twice, and Bob came out of his condo holding and petting Sir Gallagher.

"I see you're all ready to go. Where are you headed?" Bob said.

"I think I'll head up to Gallup first, then who knows?

"Stay at the El Rancho Hotel. I hear it's quite famous."

"I'll keep that in mind. Take good care of my buddy and keep an eye on my place, will you? And . . . thank you, Bob."

"No problem. But can I ask you a question?"

"Sure. You can ask me anything, friend."

"I know it's none of my business, but I wondered. You said you lost everything except your tractor. You don't have a job. So how is it that you can afford a nice condo?"

Charlie smiled at Bob's curious nature. "My mother died a few years back, and shortly after I moved here, my father passed away too. He left the farm to me, but I wasn't about to return to farming, and I sold it."

"It must have been a large farm," Bob said jokingly.

"It was substantial."

The long drive made Charlie feel relaxed. He loved the desert of southern New Mexico, and the scenery eased his mind. Charlie had read a lot about the history of the state. He looked at the landscape with amazement, the same land on which the Spanish Conquistadors once rode their horses—the *Jornada Del Muerto*, Journey of the Dead.

He thought of the Native Americans, the Apache, the Hopi, the Zuni, and the Navajo, the people who were once rulers of this land. He inserted a CD into the player and listened to his Native American flute music—the perfect music for this journey.

Exhausted, he drove into the well-lit parking lot of the Hotel El Rancho at 9:30 p.m. He hoped there would be a room available. He failed to make a reservation in his haste to leave Las Cruces. Charlie counted the number of vehicles in the parking lot. Fortunately, there weren't too many.

He could hardly keep his eyes open as he strolled into the lobby, where a half-asleep Front Desk clerk stood behind the counter.

"Do you have a single room available on the ground floor? I plan to stay in Gallup for several weeks." Charlie said.

Charlie was assigned to the first floor, room 113. He entered and immediately set the thermostat at sixty-five degrees, the best temperature for sleeping. He went directly to bed and dozed off within seconds. He woke up with a start when he heard an unusual noise. It took a few seconds before he realized he was in a hotel room and not in his bed at home. Must be a hotel guest out in the hallway, he thought. He closed his eyes and was almost asleep when he heard a loud knock on his door. He opened his eyes but didn't move. Am I dreaming, he thought. Then, another loud knock at the door. This was no dream. He jumped out of bed. Charlie opened the door wearing an olive-drab T-shirt and black sweatpants.

It was a lady in a short lavender, transparent, teddy nightgown that left little to the imagination.

"Help me," she pled. "A man just broke into my room and asked for money." Her cries and the pounding on the door alerted other guests. The hallway quickly filled up with curious on-lookers.

"Is he still in your room?" Charlie asked.

"No, I think he ran out and down the hallway, but I am not sure!"

"Wait here!" Charlie rushed to his bed, grabbed a Beretta .380 caliber pistol he kept under his pillow, and rushed out into the hallway.

"Which room?" he asked the strange woman.
She pointed down the hall. "There, the room with the opened door!"

Charlie stood next to the door. It was slightly opened. He pushed it and quickly glanced inside — nothing. He stepped into the room slowly and cautiously, eyes scanning back and forth from right to left, holding the gun tightly against his right hip. He checked the bathroom, the closet, and under the bed, but no one was there. The room was clear of intruders. He started for the door but stopped abruptly when he saw a crumpled blue paper on the floor by the door. He hadn't noticed it before, but he wasn't looking for trash — he was searching for a person.

As Charlie picked up the envelope, he heard someone whistle outside. Then, there was the discordant roar of a car, which sounded like it needed a tune-up, followed by the screeching of tires. He looked out the window and saw no movement in the parking lot.

Chile Charlie placed the crumbled paper in the pocket of his sweatpants and returned to the hallway where the strange woman was still waiting by his door. Only a handful of curious people were left in the hallway, primarily men gawking at the woman in the lavender teddy. Charlie rushed her into his room but kept the door open.

"There was no one in your room," he said. He called the Gallup Police Department and reported the attempted robbery. The dispatcher informed him that an officer would be sent.

"By the way, I'm Charlie," he said to the woman. "But everyone calls me Chile Charlie. You better stay here until the police arrive. They'll want to dust your room for fingerprints; don't want to contaminate it."

"My name is Dolly, Dolly Thompson," she said with a tremor. Her lips and chin trembled.

"Are you okay?"

"Just a bit shaken up, I guess.

Charlie glanced at her nightgown, which did not give her body much protection from the sixty-five-degree room temperature in the room, or modesty for that matter — it revealed her mature figure. Dolly became aware of her nightgown and crossed her arms in front of her with embarrassment.

"Oh, I'm sorry," Charlie said. He realized he had been staring at her body and was embarrassed. He quickly took the top blanket from his bed and placed it on Dolly's back for her to wrap around her body. There was an awkward silence for a moment.

"I was so frightened that I didn't realize I wasn't properly dressed," Dolly explained.

Charlie thought to relieve her of the embarrassment and trauma with detached conversation. He had detected a distinct Chicago nasal resonance in Dolly. "You sound like you're from Chicago."

"Why, yes," she said surprisingly.

"So, what brings you to the Land of Enchantment?"

"I'm a professor of Anthropology at Loyola University Chicago. I'm on a sabbatical to research Navajo spiritual traditions for my book. I plan to venture out in the four corners area for a few months."

"Are you Navajo?"

Dolly chuckled. It was Charlie's first honest look at her. She stood straight and seemed to have a glimpse of propriety about her. She had beautiful straight white teeth, brown eyes, straight black hair, and an aura of innocence on that forty-something face. He had already gotten a good look at her curvy, mature, and voluptuous body, but the combination of her smile, voice, and innocence made Charlie want to hug this strange woman. She was attractive, and she was black.

"No, of course, I'm not Navajo," Dolly giggled.

Twenty-five minutes later, Officer Red Shoe arrived at Charlie's room. He listened carefully and took notes as Dolly Thompson slowly reported the incident. The officer's questions conjured up the incident in her mind, and her body began to quiver, her lips trembled, and tears flowed. She was still traumatized by the stranger's abrupt entrance into her room. Her words came slowly.

"I showered around 8:15, jumped into bed, and quickly fell asleep. Then, there was a loud knock on the door. I asked, 'Who's there?' The man answered, 'Hotel Security, please open the door.'" Dolly continued. "As I opened the door, he rushed in, pushed me back, and demanded I give him money. I said, 'No,' I gave him a hard push and rushed to Charlie's door for help. That's when the man ran down the hall."

"Can you describe the intruder," Officer Red Shoe asked.

"He was around Charlie's height . . ."

"I'm almost six feet tall," Charlie said abruptly.

Dolly continued. "He had long dark brown hair with a long braided ponytail that dangled below his shoulders from the right side of his head. He appeared to be Native American."

"Can you remember what he was wearing, ma'am?" the officer asked.

"He had a red and black plaid shirt, and when he ran down the hallway, I noticed he had blue jeans and reddish-brown work-type boots." Dolly paused. "That's all I can remember."

"Thank you. We'll have a unit patrolling the area tonight," Officer Red Shoe said. In the meantime, I'm going to your room to dust the door knobs for possible fingerprints, but it doesn't sound like he was there long enough to leave any evidence."

"Wait! I just remembered," Dolly exclaimed. "When I pushed him, I noticed a small scar on the left side of his face, like a knife cut him."

Officer Red Shoe smiled. "Ma'am, around here, many men have scars like that on their faces."

Dolly and Charlie were left alone in his room. They faced each other as they attempted to gauge the other's thoughts.

"Thank you, Charlie." She smiled at him. "I think the café is still open. Maybe I can buy you a cup of coffee."

Charlie needed to be more eager. He was still tired from his trip. "How about we meet for breakfast at the hotel restaurant instead?"

Dolly accepted his invitation.

Chapter Three

Bonding

Chile Charlie had a spring in his step the following morning as he headed to the restaurant. He admired the lobby with its highly polished mahogany stairs that led to the second floor and the numerous autographed pictures of various Hollywood celebrities displayed on the walls: John Wayne, Marilyn Monroe, Clark Gable, and the like.

Charlie arrived at the café before Dolly. The walls were also plastered with pictures of notable politicians, tycoons, and Hollywood celebrities who had stayed at the hotel and eaten at the restaurant. The tables were covered with traditional red and white-checkered linen, and the legs were covered in tall cowboy boots, an unusual but nice touch. He ordered black coffee and checked the menu for *huevos rancheros*.

Dolly arrived. Charlie stood up and pulled a chair out for her. They sat across from each other.

He thought she looked much different than she did last night, more stunning.

She smiled. "Did you sleep well," she asked.

"Like a log."

Dolly ordered black coffee and studied the menu. "What are you having?"

"I am having their *huevos rancheros*." Charlie answered.

"Too spicy for me," she said. "I'm having pancakes with a sunny-side-up egg." Then, there was an awkward silence, and they looked at one another as if this was their first meeting. She thought Charlie looked different than she remembered—clean-shaven, hair combed, black jeans, a neatly pressed tan cotton shirt, and brown leather suspenders. Nice, she thought.

"Tell me about you, Charlie."

"Well, I was born in St. David, Illinois. It was a small coal-mining town comprised of 900 people of three ethnic groups—the English, the Italians, and the Croatians. I attended school there. I was good at sports and later received a scholarship to Bradley University, where I played football, baseball, and ran track. After two years of college, I joined the Army, and when I got out, I decided the best thing to do was to finish school. I got my Bachelor's and Master's degrees in education from Western Illinois University, and I ended up teaching high school and, later, seventh and eighth grades.

"During the summers, I helped my father on the family farm. I'm divorced, widowed, and have four kids . . . had four kids, but that's a different story." Charlie studied her face. "What's your story, Dolly?"

"I grew up in the Cabrini Green Housing Projects in south Chicago during the 80s and 90s. My mother was from rural Mississippi, worked in the cotton fields, and at thirteen, she was married off to the town drunk, my father. They moved to Chicago in 1986, and two years later, I was born Dolly Sweet Thompson.

I learned quickly about the hood, murder, and the mayhem there. I was eleven when I saw my first dead body. But I was one of the lucky ones. I graduated from high school and then studied Archaeology at Loyola University, emphasizing Native American Studies. And that's why I'm here."

Their meals arrived, and Charlie and Dolly continued with small talk. They finished their breakfast with additional cups of coffee and more small talk.

"Dolly, would you like to go sightseeing with me today? Gallup is known for its wonderful parks, wall paintings, and museums."

"Sure. Give me a few minutes to freshen up. I'd like to see Gallup in the light of day."

"Just knock on my door when you're ready. You know where I live," Charlie bantered.

Chapter Four

Greystone

Nate Greystone woke up to the coldness of the morning and the sound of barking dogs. He had slept in one of the back rooms of the gambling house and immediately remembered the deep trouble he was in. He had been in Gallup for three days, away from the ranch, gambling away all his money. Though usually a good gambler, his luck could have been better lately. Nate always made money with his schemes, which generally involved a crime. The police interrogated him numerous times for different crimes, but they could never pin anything on him, not even for complicity.

He grew up as a mischievous and troubled boy in the remote desert of Teec Nos Pos, Arizona. By the age of thirteen, he had been involved in one kind of trouble or another—fights, thefts, shoplifting, and constant truancy. His parents thought the evil spirits lived in him and called the *haatalii*, the medicine man, to perform the exorcism ritual to expel those spirits, but the evil spirits were too strong. The elders spoke with his parents. They did not want evil spirits in their community. Nate was sent to live with his grandparents in a far removed place near Navajo, New Mexico.

Nate had been staying at Blackrock's, a remote ranch house hidden among the hills seven miles south of Gallup. It was popular with the local criminal element and known for its gambling, drinking, drugs, prostitution, and sanctuary for young female runaways. Nate wasn't a drinker or a drug user, but he enjoyed gambling and the company of the women and other misfits.

He got up and walked towards the body of a man sleeping on the floor near his cot, with a coat draped over him like a blanket. Nate shook the man with his foot. He knew this was the safest way to wake this man. Otherwise, he may end up with a knife to his gut.

"Come on. Get up," Nate said.

The body didn't move. Nate shoved harder with his foot. "Come on, Waste Water, get up. I must go home. I need a ride."

The man moaned, turned away from Nate, and pulled his coat over his head.

"I have some information for you if you want to make money."

The man shifted into a fetal position under the coat. "Go away, leave me alone. I'm too tired, and you live too far," the man said with a groggy voice.

"Is ten thousand dollars not enough for a ride to my house?" Nate Greystone asked.

The man pushed the coat away and sprang up to a sitting position. "What are you talking about?"

"I'll tell you, Running Water, but first, take me home."

◆◆◆◆◆◆◆◆◆

Charlie and Dolly stopped at the desolate intersection of Defiance Draw Road and County Road 1 to figure out where they were and how to get to the *Tsayatoh* Government Chapter Office. They had spent three hours in the morning casually touring several sights in Gallup—the Railroad Museum, the Navajo Totem, the wall paintings in the business district that depicted the city's historical development, and the Native American Museum.

It was still early in the day, and Dolly wanted to visit the Navajo Chapter near Defiance. Charlie had decided to drive his El Camino via the scenic route north through the village of Mentmore and then west on County Road 1. They dodged in several directions throughout the sage-covered country with a sparse population of piñon trees until they arrived at the intersection.

"Charlie, are we lost," Dolly asked.

"Nope. We're not lost. I'm confused and can't get GPS on my cell phone. Service is hit and miss around here."

The driver's door was suddenly opened, and before Charlie could react, he felt the cold edge of a knife pressed against his throat. They had not seen the figure hidden in the shade of a piñon tree near the intersection.

"Lady, get out of the car and keep your hands up, and don't try anything, or you'll become a widow." The man said.

Dolly immediately exited the car, frightened, with her hands halfway up. Not again, she thought.

The assailant pressed the broad side of the blade up against the chin, forcing Charlie to tilt his head back.

"And you, white man. Come out very slowly. I don't want to hurt anybody; I want your car." He reached in and grabbed a handful of Charlie's hair with the right hand while he pressed the knife against the throat with the other. He yanked Charlie out of the car and discovered he was a tall white man. "Get down on your knees!" he ordered, pressing Charlie's head down.

"Please don't hurt him!" Dolly shouted.

The assailant turned to Dolly. "Shut up, lady, and back away from the car!"

Charlie felt the blade against his throat. He raised his left hand, pushed the assailant's hand away, grabbed the knife hand simultaneously with his right hand, and sprung up against the assailant with the quickness of a rattlesnake. Charlie spun the man around but lost his grip. The man slashed at Charlie, cut his left forearm, and turned to run. He took two steps and stopped abruptly as he faced the dark, ominous barrel of a handgun.

"Don't make me shoot you. Dolly shouted. "It won't be the first time I've killed a man! Her eyes were wide and wild, and her heart pounded hard against her chest.

The assailant turned again to run, only to meet the full force of Charlie's fist. The man went down and dropped the knife. Charlie looked at the Bowie knife with a bone handle and a wide fourteen-inch blade. Chile Charlie picked up the knife, placed the weight of his left knee on the man's chest, and pressed the blade against his throat.

"How does it feel to be on the edge of death?"

"Don't kill me! Please don't! I wasn't going to hurt anybody. I just needed the car," the assailant pleaded.

Charlie studied the man's face. He noticed the smooth dark skin and the frightened brown eyes. This was no man. This was just a boy. He yanked the boy up by the shirt collar and slammed him against the car with the forearm of the hand holding the Bowie knife. The boy wore a heavy, tan, black, wool plaid shirt under a black hoodie and an olive-drab wool coat over the hoodie.

"What's the matter with you, boy? Do you have mush for brains? You slashed at me, cut me, and you almost got yourself killed!"

Chile Charlie noticed Dolly still had the gun pointed at the boy. He nodded for her to put the gun down.

He shook the boy. "All this just for a joy ride?" Charlie was furious. His new shirt sleeve was cut and moist with blood.

"It wasn't for a joy ride," the boy said. "I just needed the car."

"What was the big hurry?"

"I need to get home to my grandmother. She's alone, and I haven't been home for a few days to help her at the ranch."

He felt like a loser; he dishonored the authentic way of Navajo. He had never committed a serious crime like this before. He was supposed to be the smart one. This wasn't how his grandparents raised him.

"All you had to do was ask for a ride." Charlie released the boy. "We'll take you home."

"It's too far, about thirty miles from here up by Crystal, east of Navajo."

"That's all right." Charlie hands him his handkerchief to wipe the blood from his nose. "What's your name, boy?"

"Nate Greystone. Everyone calls me Greystone."

"Well, Nate, do you have a sheath for this sword?"

Greystone kept his knife in an old brown leather sheath with leather stitched edges, fringes, and beadwork of turquoise, red, black, and white in the image of a Kachina's face. He reached under his opened shirt and pulled out the sheath from the inside of his belt at the small of his back.

Charlie was impressed with the leatherwork. "This is fancy leather and beadwork. Looks like something out of *Dances with Wolves*. He inserted the knife into the sheath. "Go ahead and get in the car," Charlie ordered.

"Are you going to call the police," Greystone asked.

"Only if I can get cell service, or you try something stupid again."

The boy wasn't sure what Charlie meant, but he got into the car on the passenger side.

"And don't touch anything," Charlie commanded. He walked to the back of his El Camino and motioned Dolly to join him.

"Dolly, are you all right?" He didn't wait for an answer. "I didn't know you were packing a gun."

"It's not mine. It's yours," Dolly said, "I saw you put it in the glove box this morning."

Chile Charlie had to ask. "Did you kill a man once?"

"No. I was scared and didn't know what else to say," Dolly said. She smiled. "But then, the day's still young."

Chile Charlie nodded with approval. "Thank God for the hood. Let's get out of here."

The drive was silent. Dolly sat between Charlie and Nate Greystone. She felt the warmth of Charlie's body. Nice, she thought.

Charlie drove, deep in thought. I was carjacked in broad daylight by a young Navajo punk kid in the middle of nowhere. I'm traveling with a black woman, who I just met last night and was the victim of an attempted robbery and almost killed this punk kid. And this is only my second day here. What did I get myself into? What's next?

Chapter Five

Magi Milly

Magi Milly sat on a faded red, wooden rocking chair in front of her hogan. The traditional Navajo hogan is octagonal and made of pine logs with a conical roof of mud and timber. She was a small, bony woman with a prominent chin and deep crevices on her face caused by days in the sun and age. Her gray hair was pulled back into a folded ponytail and kept behind her head with a thin leather ribbon. She wore a faded burgundy Navajo shirt and a long-sleeved velvet blouse that hung loosely on her slim body. She also wore a narrow silver bracelet and a necklace of squash blossom and turquoise. An old horse blanket draped her chair to protect her from the hardwood.

For the *Dine*—the Navajo people—the front doors always face east, so the first thing to see in the morning was the "Father Sun." For Milly, that didn't matter. She sat outside her home every morning before the light rose to the east and waited for the sun to awaken the desert. Milly watched it until it was about two fingers above the horizon, and then her day began.

Milly tended to her livestock — two horses, four cattle, and a large flock of sheep — every morning when her grandson wasn't home to help. After breakfast, she returns to her rocking chair to meditate and chant her songs until the sun becomes unbearable or something unexpected interrupts her mornings.

Charlie gazed across the landscape of red desert covered with sage and pinon trees and, farther on the horizon, to the red sandstone hills and the pine-covered slopes of the *Lukachukai* Mountains. He was astounded by the vast emptiness before him. How does one survive out here? The silliness of his question struck him. These are the Navajo people. They survived long before the white Europeans stepped foot in this country.

"So, Nate, what were you doing out here in the middle of nowhere," Charlie asked.

"I was walking home. My friend gave me a ride from Gallup, but he didn't have enough gas to take me home, so he dropped me off at the freeway, and I walked. I was resting under that tree when you showed up."

"Do you do many carjackings?" Dolly said.

"No, that was my first time," Greystone responded in a low voice, ashamed of his behavior.

His response made Dolly more curious. "Why'd you do it?"

"I needed to get home. We have a sheep ranch, and I've been gone for a while. I left my grandmother alone for three days. She has had no one else to help her since her husband died. She's very old. I guess I got scared."

His story did not move Charlie. "You're scared of an old woman? How old is she?" he asked.

"She's ninety-three."

Chile Charlie shook his head. He's afraid of an old lady, but he's brave enough to carjack us and fight me, he thought. He chuckled. "A young brave afraid of a ninety-three-year-old woman."

"You don't know my grandmother," he growled.

Greystone directed Charlie onto a dirt road and traveled several more miles. "I see my Hogan," Greystone said as he pointed in the direction.

"A hogan?" Charlie said, surprised. "I've never seen a real hogan." He looked hard but only saw two stunted Juniper trees in the distance.

Dolly could not see it either. "Are you sure, Greystone," Dolly asked.

"Just follow the road," Greystone said.

Chile Charlie was curious to see a Navajo hogan. He was aware that Hogan meant *earth home* in the *Dine* language. He had seen them in movies and pictures in history class, but this was the first time he had visited one.

They arrived. An authentic hogan with smoke billowing through a stack stood on a hill in the flat valley. It was surrounded by corrals, a stable with horses, an outhouse, and an old 1970 Ford truck. It was like one of those pictures he had seen on *Arizona Highways* and *New Mexico* magazine.

Milly sat rocking in her chair outside next to the east door when the El Camino arrived. She looked

42

uncomfortable and bewildered at seeing her grandson with an uninvited guest.

Nate quickly got out of the car. He was happy to see his grandmother, but she did not look happy. Though Greystone was twenty, she still worried about him. She had raised him in the traditional ways of the Navajo to maintain a *Balance of Life*, even if there was a wrong, and with her grandson, there was always evil.

"Young Owl, where have you been? Why were you gone so long? I needed your help." A frown appeared on her dark, weather-beaten face. "You should not be gone for so long."

"But, Grandma, it was only three days. I was in Gallup, and I couldn't get a ride back home," he explained with his eyes cast to the ground.

"Yes, but the sheep needed to be tended. That's how we survive, and I have no one else to help. You know that."

"I'm sorry, Grandmother," he said with remorse.

Charlie and Dolly watched the chastisement. They slowly exited the car with embarrassed smiles.

The old woman remained stoic and eyed them for a moment. A tall white man and a black woman, this is a sign, she thought. She turned her eyes to the desert and scanned the sky, then the land. "Look," she said to the strangers as she pointed to several dust funnels moving about in the desert. "Devils dancing in the wind. You never know what the spirits will bring next," she said.

"My name is Charlie, and this is Dolly." He didn't know what to make of this old woman, but he spoke reverently.

"I am Magi Milly. Why does my grandson have blood on his face, and why have you blood on your arm?"

"It was a misunderstanding," Charlie said. He removed the sheath with the Bowie knife from his belt and handed it to the old woman. "This belongs to your grandson."

Milly takes the knife and stares at it. "This was a gift to Young Owl from his grandfather. His great-grandfather made it." She turns to her grandson.

"Young Owl, go tend to the horses," she commanded.

Milly walked directly to the door and motioned Charlie and Dolly to join her. She walked with a four-foot staff of mesquite wood with leather wrapping adorned with turquoise beads, two silver jingle bells, and two hawk feathers.

The structures haven't changed much from earlier times, Dolly thought. She guessed the hogan was about twenty-five feet in diameter. She also took note of the construction — the eight-inch diameter post at each point of the octagon, the chinking in the gaps between the pine logs, and the pole rafters that make up the conical roof. She wanted to take pictures for her book but did not want to offend Milly.

Charlie was impressed and in awe of Milly's home. An old flat-top iron stove with wood burning and crackling in the firebox sat at the west end, vented with a stovepipe that rose through the roof. There were no pictures on the wall, just sand paintings, a dry sheepskin, dreamcatchers, and Indian blankets hung on several wood racks. There were two twin beds, one on the north and the other on the south. Lever action .30-.30 caliber rifles hung on a gun rack on the wall above one of the beds. A dresser and a nightstand stood on the side of each bed, and along the southeastern wall was a worn-out, burgundy leather couch with a mesquite wood coffee table in front. Carpets of earth-tone colors covered the aged and squeaky wood floor planks.

Charlie noticed the wood shelves with several sticks of cut sage and jars filled with what appeared to be herbs or spices—he wasn't sure.

They sat on a willow log bench and table in the middle of the house. Magi Milly poured coffee and sat across from the strange guest. She reached into her pocket, removed a smoking pipe, and struck a match against her leather belt to light it. She breathed in and exhaled the smoke from her nostrils and sat relaxed. "Thank you for bringing Young Owl home. It is important to have him here."

"Why do you call him 'Young Owl'? I thought his name was Nate," Charlie said.

Milly looked out the window on the north side, where she could see Young Owl combing one of the horses. "He is wise but too young to know it, she explained. "It is the war name given when young. It's the only name that counts and is kept secret within the family. The name is only used in one's *Blessing Way Ceremony* or when a Singer performs a cure.

" Milly puffed on her pipe. "Young Owl visits too often with the black hearts," she said as she continued to look out the window. She turned and noticed the confused looks of her guest.

"Other boys whose hearts are black and evil," Milly explained. "I see the good spirit in Young Owl, but I have not been able to make it appear. When he was sent to me by his parents, I gave him a medicine bag to always carry with him. I hoped it would keep his evil spirits away." She glances out the window again. "He keeps it hidden inside his pants as if he were ashamed of his Navajo heritage."

Milly surprised Chile Charlie. For an old woman, she was well-spoken and spry, not feeble, nor spoke with an old gruff voice.

"Well, Magi Milly, don't worry. We're not calling the police on Young Owl. I'm sure he's a good kid and doesn't need more problems."

Nate Greystone walked into the house and poured himself a cup of coffee. "It's cold outside," he announced.

"Young Owl, you need to thank our guest and apologize. They are not calling the Tribal Police."

"Thank you, Mr. Charlie . . ."

"Charlie. Everyone calls me Chile Charlie, but you can call me Charlie."

"Thank you both. I'm sorry for my bad behavior. I will pay the hospital bill for your cut and buy you a new shirt."

"Don't worry about it. It's just a scratch, and this is an old shirt anyway."

"Is Chile Charlie your war name," Milly asked.

"Grandma, white men don't get war names," Greystone interrupted, "but Chile Charlie does sound good."

Everyone laughed except Milly. "Mr. Charlie, I can see your good spirit but troubles in your eyes."

"It's probably from the wind and sand," he said jokingly to conceal his embarrassment.

"Your eyes speak, and I hear them," Milly told him.

Charlie didn't know how to respond. This is a strange woman. We need to go, he thought. He averted his eyes towards Dolly and then back to Milly. "I think it's time for us to go. We've intruded enough . . ."

"Listen to her, Mr. Charlie," Nate blurted out, "She may be an old woman, but she is very wise. She knows things."

"Well, it's getting late, and we need to get to the *Tsayatoh* office before they close," Charlie said.

"Yes, I'm a professor from a university in Chicago and doing comparative research on tribal rituals. I hope to get information and some leads from the tribal chapters," Dolly said.

She explained her reason for coming to New Mexico and shared the incident at the El Rancho Hotel. When she gave them the description of the suspect, Milly and Nate made subtle glances at each other.

"Charlie, where are you from," Milly asked.

"I live in Las Cruces now." He explained how he arrived in the Land of Enchantment.

"Why are you here, in the reservations?" Milly asked.

"I just thought I'd get to know the country better and clear my head," Charlie said.

"Clear your head from your trouble? That's why you come to see Magi Milly," she stated.

"No. I was told to find a priest from one of the old missions or a shaman from the reservation to help me with some mystical therapy. Do you know where I can find one? He chuckled to make light of the conversation.

"Grandmother knows of many Shamans," Nate Greystone said.

"Your grandmother knows Shaman?" Chile Charlie asked surprisingly.

Greystone looked at his grandmother, then back at Charlie. "She is Shaman."

Milly inhaled deeply from her pipe. She held the smoke momentarily, then blew it upwards slowly until her lungs were empty. Milly concentrated intently on the smoke as if she saw something in it. She glanced directly at Charlie with her dark brown eyes. "Chile Charlie, come with me."

Milly signaled Greystone with her eyes to stay with Dolly, then walked out the door. Charlie curiously obeyed and followed her outside to the edge of an overlook behind the hogan.

Scanning the open land and the red cliffs on the southern horizon, Milly pointed to the desert with her staff. "Everything that makes the people comes from Mother Earth. People must find balance by becoming one with her." Milly said.

"So, I need to find the Navajo Middle Way Balance?" Charlie asked.

"You need to purify your body and cleanse the bad spirit from your mind. Then, you must learn to become one with Mother Earth."

"How do I purify myself and become one with the earth," He asked.

"I will prepare the ceremony for you. Come back in three days. Bring only the clothes you wear and a blanket. When the healing occurs, you will be alone for three days with Mother Earth. You will get to know her."

Chapter Six

Blue Notes

Greystone rode horseback as he escorted Charlie and Dolly to Indian Service Route 12, the main road that would take them back to Interstate 40. It was past 4:00 p.m. and too late to stop at the *Tsayatoh* Chapter Office. It was closed.

Chile Charlie and Dolly were back at the restaurant of the El Rancho Hotel by early evening. Dolly had a glass of cabernet wine, and Charlie had a prickly pear margarita.

"Did you notice how Milly and Greystone looked at each other when I mentioned the robber's description," Dolly asked.

"I did, and that reminds me, I found a blue crumpled-up note on the floor in your room last night. I forgot to give it to you."

"It's not mine," Dolly said. "What did it say?"

"I don't know. I thought it was yours, and I wasn't about to pry. It's in the pocket of my sweatpants."

Dolly and Charlie stared at one another. "The robbers!" they said collectively.

"He must've dropped it when I shoved him!" Dolly exclaimed.

"Shhh, we don't want the whole world to know," Charlie warned.

They finished their drinks and walked briskly to Charlie's room.

Charlie went to the closet where he had left his sweatpants. He took the note out of his pocket. They both sat on the edge of the bed as Charlie unfolded the note. It was a light blue, four-inch square, a ruled paper that looked like it had been ripped from a notepad. Dolly leaned into Charlie, almost cheek to cheek, to read the note. It was scribbled in black ink.

waste water   house Tohatchi tomorrow 7pm see li

"What do you make of it, Charlie?

"Whoever wrote this note can't spell or punctuate. Looks like he was in a hurry, not sure, though."

He studied the note further. "Waste water . . ." he pauses to think. "He must be a plumber, or he works on septic systems. Waste water is also called grey water, which means it's an RV or a mobile home."

"It says house."

"For some people, an RV is a house."

"We need to give this note to the police," Dolly suggested.

"We don't have time for that. It's 6:30 now. That means the robber is on his way to Tohatchi right now. Can you identify him if we see him?"

"I'm sure I can. Let's go!" Dolly said. "Wow, this is like the movies."

They arrived in Tohatchi at 7:12 p.m. and began their search at the north side of the town by the high school.

"What are we looking for, Charlie," Dolly asked.

"People working outside on a septic system or anyone walking around outside. I want to find the man who tried to rob you."

They saw no signs of human activity, and the suspect would have been difficult to recognize if there were any. The town was dark, except for a few dim street lights, and the lights turned on inside houses with closed shades. Chile Charlie returned to Highway 491 and headed to the south part of the town, which was even darker than the north side. They drove on the paved road past several houses and the Tohatchi Chapter building until they came to a Y-intersection. To the right was a dark cul-de-sac, and to the left was a dirt road with a few houses. Charlie turned left. They were several yards up the road when the front end of the El Camino began to shake. Charlie stopped to check.

"Well, our adventure is over. I got a flat tire on the front left side."

"You need some help?"

"No, but you can keep me company. Don't worry about snakes out here. It's too cold for them. You won't see them till spring."

Just then, Charlie heard an engine roar and an even louder bang that echoed throughout the small community.

"Is someone shooting," Dolly asked with concern. She had grown up where loud bangs were heard almost nightly, a signal that usually meant someone was injured or killed.

"No, that sounded like a backfire from a car. I guess people around here have something against car tune-ups. It sounded like they were in some hurry, too." Then, it struck him. "Damn! That might've been our boy."

Chapter Seven

Tribal Meeting

Jimmy Running Water drove his truck into the parking lot and parked next to a white SUV with its engine running. A man sat alone, smoking a cigarette in the dark. The only ambient light came from neighboring buildings.

Jimmy got out of his truck and approached the driver. "Are you Li?"

The man got out of the SUV. He was slender, medium height, short grey hair, and wore black rim glasses. "You must be Running Water," he stated.

"Maybe, if your name is Li."

"I understand you and your partner have something for me," he said.

He sounds educated, Jimmy thought. "We do."

"I have a buyer for the antiquities. He'll be here on the eleventh. You'll receive the standard three percent fee. That's over ten thousand dollars each for you and your associate, minus the one thousand dollars fee from each of you for my messenger."

A fee? The imposed fee did not sit well with Jimmy. "We were told we'd be getting ten thousand dollars each. There was no mention of a messenger's fee."

"That's the cost of doing business."

"We were promised ten thousand, and that's what we want," Jimmy insisted.

"You don't understand business. It's called paying commissions. That's what I'm doing, paying you a commission, and you must pay a commission to the man who got you this job.

Jimmy sensed this man was attempting to cheat him. "That's not our problem!"

Li was growing impatient with this ignorant boy. "If it weren't for the messenger, you wouldn't get the job in the first place, and I'm sure nine thousand dollars is more than you have now. Just remember, I control all the money."

"You forget one thing, Li. You may control the money, but we control the masks; without them, you won't have any money to control. How's that for understanding business?"

Li realized the risk. He could lose the whole deal to this petty thief. "Don't be so rash. I'll tell you what. I will pay you the full commission, and you can pay the messenger yourself. How does that sound?" Li guessed that the messenger would never see the money from Jimmy and his partner, but they eventually would pay for that.

"That sounds like good business to me," Jimmy agreed.

"I want them delivered on the morning of the eleventh," Li said sternly. "The buyer will be here with cash. I'll send all the information . . . with the messenger." Li grinned.

A car passed by slowly heading west. Neither man spoke nor moved. The backlights turned into bright red lights when the passing car was about four blocks away.

"It stopped," Li said. "I think it's time for us to vanish."

Running Water rushed to his truck. He shifted into reverse, backed up, then shifted into first gear and sped away in the darkness with his headlights turned off.

Chapter Eight

First Day

Three days passed, and Milly sat on her rocking chair, puffing on her pipe, waiting. The sun had just risen above the horizon when Chile Charlie and Dolly arrived at the hogan as requested.

"You don't suppose they'll have me stand in the sun for twenty-four hours straight with just my skivvies on, stick eagle's talons and rock skewers through my chest skin, and then have me hanging to the lodge pole by leather straps, do you?" Charlie said.

Dolly broke into a burst of laughter. "Someone's been watching *A Man Called Horse* too many times." The laughter continued. "Oh, Charlie, it's just a purification ceremony to help you rid your mind of the 'bad spirits.' You're not taking a vow or becoming a warrior. Besides, the Sun Dance Ritual has been outlawed since 1883, and it was never a Navajo ritual. It was the Plains Indians'." Charlie felt embarrassed about his ignorance and lack of research on the topic. "Well, I still like to watch *A Man Called Horse*. It's a classic."

Dolly hugged Charlie, wished him luck, and drove away. She had made copies of Google Maps at the hotel and navigated her way to Interstate 40 and back to Gallup without a problem.

Charlie brought a blanket from his hotel bed.

"That won't do," Milly told him. She walked into the hogan.

Shortly after, Nate Greystone came out carrying a large, thick wool Indian blanket—dark brown with rust stripes delineated with thin tan lines. "Here, this will keep you warm," Greystone said. "It's eighty-one years old. Grandmother made it when she was twelve." He traded blankets with Charlie.

Milly came out of the hogan, holding the keys to her truck. "The sweat lodge at Oak Creek is several miles away. We will have the purification ceremony there. Young Owl has already prepared the sweat lodge," Magi Milly said.

Greystone drove the truck while Charlie sat between him and Milly. Chile Charlie was a bit apprehensive and still uncertain about what would happen. He had expressed his grave concern to Dolly about the night before.

The three arrived at the base of the canyon, to an open area surrounded by dead juniper trees. The sweat lodge was a dome structure ten feet in diameter and five feet high made of mud and tree branches. The interior was completely dug out about a foot and a half deep and filled with river rock up to the ground level, except for a circular, two-foot opening in the center containing a firewood pile. The top surface of the piled rock was covered with dried mud, five inches deep, to protect a person from the hot rocks. A large wood tub, made from the bottom half of a wine barrel, filled with water from the Oak Creek, lay inside the lodge.

Greystone built a fire, and as the stones heated, he poured water over the hot rocks with a large wooden spoon. Steam began to rise. Meanwhile, Chile Charlie waited outside until Nate was done with the preparations.

"If you are ready, we will begin with the purification ceremony. You'll need to strip," Magi Milly explained.

Chile Charlie removed his clothing, including a new pair of thermal long johns he wore over a black pair of jogging shorts, which he did not remove. Milly began the ritual with chants and songs, followed by prayers that symbolized the call to the Gods of the Four Directions. She sprayed Charlie with a special cleansing liquid composed of sage, water, and plants of the desert. She held the burning sage before Charlie and told him to wave the smoke onto him.

"The entrance of the sweat lodge represents innocence and rebirth," Milly explained. "To enter the sweat lodge, you are required to get on your hands and knees as an act of humility while symbolically reentering the womb of our Great Mother Earth. Mother Earth knows your deepest wounds and needs and how to resolve them, and she requires absolute humility, vulnerability, and honesty."

Charlie entered the lodge alone on his hands and knees, then sat on the bare mud, a natural connection to Mother Earth herself. It was dark, and the only light came from the burning logs and the hole in the ceiling for the smoke to escape. Milly picked up a door, a frame of tree branches covered with sheepskin, and placed it over the entrance.

"Keep pouring water on the rocks," Milly said to Charlie. She continued her chants as she pounded her staff on the red earth with a rhythmic beat, which made the jingle bells sound more like a tambourine, while Greystone beat on a small drum and chanted along.

Beads of sweat began to pour out of Charlie's body. He poured water over the rocks. Steam instantly filled the lodge with a thick mist. Sweat ran down his forehead and burned his eyes. He bent forward so the beads of sweat fell directly on the earth. The wide steam was almost suffocating, and he coughed. Exhaustion set in, and he felt like he was about to pass out. He concentrated on the chants, the beat of the drum, and the bells whir, which made him enter a state of euphoria.

Chile Charlie had no idea how long he had been in the lodge. His mind wandered in a dream-like state. He saw the buffalo, the Anasazi people, a lone coyote in the desert, and a wide river. Then he saw the snow in the desert and felt the chill of a cold winter.

"Charlie, it is time to leave the sweat lodge," Milly said as she opened the door and let the cool air in.

Charlie crawled out, and the cool air felt good on his body. Greystone handed him a towel to dry off the sweat. Charlie dressed, Greystone extinguished the fire, and they left the sweat lodge site.

"Was that it?" Charlie asked.

"No. It is now time to start your journey," Milly said.

◆◆◆◆◆◆◆◆◆◆

They arrived at a canyon of red sandstone walls east of Navajo, New Mexico. They got out of the truck. Charlie looked at the land.

"The canyon is impressive," Charlie said in a hushed voice. "What's this place?"

"This is the land of the ancients who mysteriously disappeared from the desert. Much later, it became the land of our ancestors, the *Dine*. The ground is filled with their blood, and their spirits roam this land.

"You must learn to avoid extremes. All does not exist," she said in a firm voice. "You must take the time to learn the intricacies and complexities of Mother Earth. This will take three days, and it starts here.

"The Navajo ritual, known as the *night chant*, is a healing ceremony lasting for three days and nights. It is performed in winter to restore the order and balance of human relationships within the Navajo universe. It includes praying, sacred dances, blessings, and chants. You will remain in this land of our ancestors, but you will not be alone. Mother Earth will be with you. Head into the canyon and wander the land. Observe the sky, the creatures, and the vegetation. Find the balance. It will help you find the peace and harmony you seek."

Milly walked to the truck and retrieved a leather bag from the back of the passenger's seat. She took out the sheath with the large Bowie knife and handed it to Charlie. "Take this. You will need it for your journey."

Charlie took the knife and glanced over to Greystone, who nodded approvingly.

"We will return to this spot four days from now."

"What am I supposed to do?" Charlie asked.

"Find a center and travel from there."

Charlie wasn't sure what that meant. Perhaps she was talking metaphorically, he thought.

Milly and Greystone left without another word, and Charlie was alone with Mother Earth.

The canyon was spotted with melting snow from a previous snowfall that covered most of northern New Mexico at the higher elevations from Santa Fe to southern Colorado and barely touched west as far as Chinle, Arizona. It was already past noon when Charlie started on his journey. He walked down a slope to the flat land between two canyon walls. He wasn't sure what to do for the next three days and nights other than to 'become one with the earth.' His only certainty was finding a water source and a place to keep warm against the cold nights.

Water was the priority. Charlie knew a man could survive a week or more without food but only three days without water — a lesson he learned from his grandfather when Charlie was a young boy. For many years, during his youth, he and his grandfather camped in the wilderness during deer seasons. Young Charlie then learned survival skills — to hunt, find food from the land, make a fire, and most importantly, always find water first.

Worst case scenario, I can eat snow, Chile Charlie thought. He continued to walk northeast and occasionally looked back to mark his trail for his return trip to where Magi Milly would meet him. After forty minutes of walking on the arid, rocky terrain, he finally found a water source—a runoff of melting snow from the top of a mesa of Bowl Canyon down a gully. It was good, clean water. Charlie drank as much as his body could handle to keep him going until the next day. He decided to stay within proximity of the gully and to venture just far enough without the risk of dehydration.

He continued to journey the canyon until he spotted a location on the southern slope. It was a shallow cavity carved into the red sandstone by the winds of time, with a rocky overhang above that would protect it from the rain or snow. He climbed the slope to examine the cave. It wasn't large, but it was deep enough to protect him from the weather and maintain a fire that would radiate against the stone wall to keep him warm. The floor was solid sandstone, and the ceiling was nearly five feet high, not enough to stand in but sufficient to sit and sleep. It was perfect, he thought—a place where he could hold out for three days.

Chile Charlie wiped the dust and small stones from the floor and placed the large wool blanket down. He walked down the slope and walked a distance, collecting dead branches from juniper pine trees and dried pinion leaves and pine needles. He collected a substantial pile to build a fire to warm him well into the following day. He was getting hungry but was too tired to hunt for food.

He sat on the blanket, cut a notch into a thick tree branch with the Bowie knife, then stripped a thin branch and rounded the tip. He placed the stick into the notch and rubbed it back and forth between his palms. It's an old Indian trick to start a fire, his grandfather had told Charlie. He kept rubbing for an extended amount of time. Finally, smoke. He placed a few dried leaves on top of the notch and continued to rub the thin branch on the log. Like a miracle, he had a fire. He added more dry twigs until he had a good fire going. The trick was to keep the ambers hot enough throughout the night to make it easier to start the next day's fire.

The cave warmed up. Charlie sat on the Indian blanket and watched the desert below. Three vultures circled over the canyon. A dead animal, Charlie thought. Darkness and cold set in early. Charlie sat on the edge of the large wool blanket, reached back, and pulled it over himself. It wasn't long before he closed his eyes and fell asleep sitting with his legs crossed.

Chapter Nine

Second Day

Dolly Thompson drove to Albuquerque to meet with Dr. Levi Garcia, Professor of Southwestern Native American Studies at the University of New Mexico. It was 'Finals Week,' and she had only a few days before the university closed for the Christmas break.

She sat at his office and discussed possibly joining the archeological dig at Canyon de Chelly as an observer and conducting interviews for her book.

"I'm sorry, Miss Thompson, but that project has been shut down indefinitely," Dr. Garcia said.

"Why is that?"

"I am not at liberty to say, just that we encountered some difficulties that we have to sort out, but we can certainly accommodate you at Chaco Canyon."

Dolly was curious about Canyon de Chelly. Still, she was glad to be able to be part of the Chaco Canyon project. "Thank you, professor. I appreciate that."

"You're welcome. We're always happy to help a colleague interested in the Native American culture."

She changed the subject. "What do you make of this break-in at the Native American Museum in Gallup?

Professor Garcia raised an eyebrow at Dolly as if surprised by her question. "That is an odd case, a break-in without taking anything. I know the curator from there, Dr. Acothley. He is meticulous in his work. He would know immediately if any was missing."

"I suppose they're still checking their inventory to find out if anything is missing," Dolly said.

"So, how are you enjoying the southwest so far? The professor asked.

Dolly told him about the attempted robbery on her first night and the carjacking the following morning.

"Don't you carry any protection with you," Dr. Garcia asked.

"No, I never needed to, and I'm from Chicago." She laughed.

"I guess you've already learned it's still the Wild West out here." He chuckled. "You know, there's a gun show here in town this weekend. You should probably go there. Maybe you'll find something that suits you."

◆◆◆◆◆◆◆◆◆◆

It was still dark when Charlie woke up to the sounds of chirping birds as if to announce the coming of Father Sun. He was lying on the ground feeling cold; the fire had gone out, but the occasional wind into the cave kept the wood red.

Charlie grabbed a handful of thin twigs and dried leaves and placed them over the hot logs. He blew on them until the leaves hissed into a flame. He put bigger branches on top and started a decent fire. Light began to silhouette the mountains to the east, and dark gray clouds began to take on a combination of lavender, mauve, and blue hues above the sun. The combination of the sunrise and the cool, fragrant desert air gave Charlie a strange sensation, but he would not move until it was warm enough to go out into the canyon. The clouds scudded away like ghosts, fading into nothing in the wind. Father Sun finally appeared.

He hadn't eaten in the past twenty-four hours, and the pain of hunger gnawed at his stomach. The Canyon was bleak and nearly bare of vegetation—no McDonalds. What could I round up to eat? Charlie gazed around. A lone eagle flew over the canyon to the east. Maybe it spotted some food. He threw more twigs into the fire to keep it going, then scuttled down the slope. Halfway down, he spotted a coyote heading east. Maybe it's going after the same food, he thought. The coyote stopped and turned its head in Charlie's direction. Charlie froze in place, hoping not to frighten it away. The coyote continued walking leisurely, not bothered by a man's presence. The eagle soared almost directly above Charlie. The coyote suddenly burst into a full run to the south and up a hill, where it stopped at the crest, turned to look at Charlie momentarily, and disappeared over the hill. I must've scared it off, Charlie thought.

The cold yielded to the warmth of the sun. Charlie continued east on the sand and rocky terrain and walked around clumps of small pinyon junipers that looked more like bushes than trees. As he glanced up the canyon, a mountain cottontail rabbit took a startling dash from under a bush and ran north across Charlie's path. It hid under another Pinyon tree about fifty yards away. Charlie stopped for a moment. He followed the cotton tail slowly, but it ran farther away as Charlie approached. He could not get close enough to catch his breakfast. If I miss this one, I might go hungry for the rest of the day or days.

The rabbit ran towards the north wall of the canyon. Charlie thought he'd have only two ways to go if I could get him to run to the wall. The rabbit headed for the canyon wall and stopped to figure out his next move. Charlie picked up a rock the size of a baseball and continued toward his prey. The rabbit ran east along the wall past an enormous Pinyon tree in front of the wall. Charlie estimated his windage, threw the rock as hard as possible, and struck the back of the rabbit's head. It continued for a few feet and then balled up and squirmed. Charlie ran behind the rabbit's trail. His eyes were focused on the squirming creature, and he did not see the two bowling ball-sized rocks on the ground before him. He tripped, flew forward, and crashed on the graveled ground. As is human nature, he looked back to see what caused his fall. He thought the two rocks looked out of place. At least I got my usual run this morning, he thought. He got up, breathing hard, and walked to the motionless rabbit — it was dead.

Charlie picked up his breakfast and walked back to the unusual rocks. He didn't know what to make of them. Was it some marker? Indians were known to mark their trails, but this was no trail. Charlie squatted next to the rocks and examined them. One had crusted red dirt embedded in the crevices on the top side. He stood up and searched the nearby area. He found two impressions on the ground where the rocks once rested. From where he stood and from the direction of the sunlight, he noticed the difference in the top soils. It was less grainy around the rocks than the rest of the terrain. He examined the ground around the rocks. It was softer. Something had been recently buried here, he thought. He left the area to prepare breakfast but planned to return later.

Charlie skinned the rabbit and removed the entrails before he returned to his cave to avoid uninvited wildlife and insects where he slept. He gathered extra wood for his campfire. He skewered the rabbit with a long, thin, and almost straight branch and placed the ends on stacked flat sandstone rocks, which he happened to put on opposite sides of the fire so the rabbit would cook above the flame. Chile Charlie took his time to roast his lunch. He knew two things about the desert rabbit—never eat them before the first frost, and rabbit meat needs to cook for at least two hours. The frost kills the fleas and ticks that carry Lyme disease, and they will not taste gamey and leathery if simmered.

The first bite of the rabbit was not what he expected. It was a bit tough, but it would keep him nourished. Charlie kept thinking about the strange rocks he tripped over and wondered what was beneath the ground. It couldn't be a sacred burial ground. The hole appeared to be square-shaped and not rectangular. It couldn't be a body, and it couldn't be ancient because it was freshly dug. The thoughts about the strange hole fed his curiosity while the cooked rabbit fed his body.

He ate half of the rabbit and thought to save the other half for the next day. He took it further up to the top of the slope, where there were large patches of snow. Charlie built a mound of snow, placed the remaining rabbit on top, and built another large pile of snow over it. With his Bowie knife, he cut several branches of juniper with leaves and placed them over his mound of snow. He hoped a coyote, bobcat, or mountain lion wouldn't discover tomorrow's breakfast.

He was sure he could locate the two strange rocks again, but he had to return to the gully to fill himself with enough water to hold him over for another day.

♦♦♦♦♦♦♦♦♦♦

Charlie got on his hands and knees and examined the ground. Yes, someone recently dug this hole, but why, and what? "We're about to find out."

Charlie looked for a large, flat sandstone rock for digging. He found one and pounded a beveled edge on one side for digging and scooping.

The deeper he dug, the softer the soil. He dug and scooped until he was a foot down — nothing. He continued to scoop. Two feet deep and still nothing. The sun was warming, and Chile Charlie began to sweat. He removed his coat and proceeded to dig and scoop. Three feet into the hole, and still, there was nothing.

"This must be something large and serious," Charlie said. He was sweating profusely. His breathing was heavy, and he sat for a rest. He was glad he drank a lot of water. Still, he wished he had a canteen. A prickly pear margarita sounded good about now. He dug again. His sweat dripped into the soil, his shoulder and arm muscles began to burn, and his palms began to blister. Charlie was persistent. He scraped with the flat rock and lifted loose dirt out of the hole with cupped hands until, finally, a black cloth appeared. He stood up to catch his breath and scanned his surroundings to ensure no one was watching. He looked at the sky, hoping for clouds, but all he saw in the pale blue was the eagle soaring high above him. Maybe he's thinking of making a meal of me, Charlie thought.

To avoid damage to whatever was down there, he carefully dug around the cloth with his hands and scooped the dirt away methodically like a professional archeologist. Within moments, he located the collar of a black cloth sack, wrapped tightly with a long and thin leather strap. He dug along the sides and soon discovered it was a large sack. He scooped dirt out until he could lift the bag from the hole by its collar. He untied the strap and looked inside and saw some things individually wrapped in red velvet cloth. He took one from the bag and unfolded the cloth. It was a Kachina mask made of old dried leather, painted in several colors that had long ago lost its luster.

A sense of excitement came over him, as well as a sense of fear. Many thoughts whirled in his head like dirt devils, mainly because he had broken a taboo law. Is this something man was not meant to find, he thought. He felt a sudden sense that someone was watching him. He looked in all directions, but there was no one—only the eagle above him.

Charlie wrapped the mask and placed it back in the bag. This is nothing mystical, he thought. These are just stolen relics, most likely from the museum. He recalled, from the news, that no items were reported missing. Charlie covered the hole and placed the original rocks over it. He carried the sack away, along with his digging rock, back to his cove.

The gully still ran with clear water, and Charlie drank as much as possible to replace what he had lost that morning. He decided to hide the black sack somewhere near the gully as it was closer to the trail where Milly was to pick him up.

Charlie searched the area for an inconspicuous hiding place. He decided that the best site would be up on the slope. He spotted a good location, behind the third juniper tree west of the gully. Charlie carefully removed rocks and dug a shallow hole wide and deep enough for easy recovery. He covered the hole with moist soil and spread dry dirt for concealment. He placed the original rocks over the hole — it looked untouched. No one would suspect that hiding behind a tree, up on a slope, is a hole containing valuable Indian artifacts. He drank more cool water and returned to his cave.

Chapter 10

Third Day

Charlie woke up hungry and tired but decided not to eat the rabbit again. Let nature have that rabbit, he thought. He returned to the gully and discovered it was drying up. The warm sun had melted away most of the snow from the top of the mesa. There was still some water to drink, but there might be none by tomorrow. He thought Milly would be here in twenty-four hours to pick me up and return me to civilization.

Chile Charlie spends his last day walking about the desert. He appreciated the beauty of the sky, the land formations, the flora, and what little wildlife he saw — mostly lizards and a few ground squirrels that came out to bask in the sun's warmth. What am I doing here? What is it that I am supposed to see that would make my life clear, he wondered. In the evening, he gathered dry wood and returned to his cave.

The canyon began to cool. He started a campfire near the edge of the overhang above the cove. He sat close to the fire, wrapped with the old Indian blanket over his head. He thought about the black sack and the Kachina masks. Where did they come from? Who hid them in the canyon, and why? Should I report them to the police? What if the feds take them just like they confiscated the T-Rex fossil from the Lakota tribe in South Dakota? It was never seen again. Those masks belong to the people of the local tribes.

Magi Milly would return in eighteen hours. He was there to learn about the Navajo Way, not to retrieve lost treasures. Should I tell her about what I found or hide it from Magi? Although he had secured the Kachina masks, he needed to figure out if he was doing the right thing. He grew exhausted and didn't think about it any longer. He waited for the early sunset of late fall and observed the canyon silently, without motion. He returned to his cave and fell asleep.

◆◆◆◆◆◆◆◆◆◆

Chile Charlie woke up as the bright sun peeked out of the eastern sky. He was anxious to leave the canyon. He cleaned out the cave and left no trace that he had been there. He rolled up his blanket and walked past the gully. It was dry.

Magi Milly and Greystone waited in the truck, and he was happy to see them. Greystone handed him a jug of fresh water from Oak Creek, which Charlie almost emptied with large gulps. The return trip to the hogan was quiet. Milly didn't ask about his experience, and Greystone just smiled.

They arrived at Milly's home, where Dolly waited by the El Camino. She had a pleasant smile. "Hello, Chile Charlie."

"How are you, Dolly?"

"I'm glad you're back safe and sound. Are you okay?" Dolly asked. "I bet you're ready to return to the hotel for a hot shower and lunch."

Charlie nodded eagerly. "Yes, I want a shower, food, and a soft bed, in that order."

Charlie shook hands with Nate Greystone. He turned to Milly.

"Thank you, Magi Milly. I will never forget this experience." He handed the Bowie knife back to her.

"Goodbye, Chile Charlie. Go home and rest," Milly said. She walked into the hogan without another word.

Charlie and Dolly drove away.

"How was your experience in the canyon?"

"Dolly, you will not believe what I found." He told her about accidentally tripping over the two rocks and discovering a hidden treasure.

Chapter Eleven

Strange Friends

John Trefren sat at the El Ranch Hotel restaurant having breakfast with his old friend, Russell Strongbow, reminiscing and laughing about their youth's mischief, some of which amounted to petty crimes.

"Remember when Officer Kelso ran after those kids at the shopping center? He left his police car running with the flashing red and blue overhead lights, and you went to his car and locked it. We sat in your GTO and watched old "Fat" Kelso run back to get into his car, and he couldn't get in!" Russell broke into loud laughter.

"I was just a punk juvenile back then. I'm just lucky I never got caught," Trefren said.

"I can't believe you did all those things back then, Trefren," Russell Strongbow said, shaking his head.

"And here you are, a detective with the Gallup Police Department."

Trefren was a medium-sized man, about five-foot-nine, with deep-set eyes on his narrow oval face. A few strands of gray highlighted his thick, dark hair. He was a fifteen-year veteran of the Gallup Police Department—the last nine years spent as a detective working in the Felony Crimes Division. Only relatives and close friends called him *Tre*. He was from the Ramah Navajo Reservation north of Gallup.

His friend, Russell Strongbow, was from the neighboring Zuni reservation northeast of Gallup. He was a tall, barrel-chested, and muscular man with long black hair split in the center and always wore a broad red headband to hold his hair in place, which made him look more Apache than Zuni. Russell was proud of his body and wore tight-fitted shirts to show off his muscular physique and jeans so tight against his body that it left little to the imagination.

The two had been friends since childhood, and even though Russell served five years in the State prison in Santa Fe for armed robbery and assault with a deadly weapon, they continued as close friends.

"So, Russ, what did you want to see me about? Trefren asked.

"I'm missing some sheep and a few goats, and I think I know who the thieves are. It's that Nate Greystone and his two buddies, Jimmy Running Water and Chris Leaping Bear," Russell said, pounding his forefinger on the table.

"What makes you believe they're responsible," Trefren asked.

"Everyone knows they're the biggest thieves in the whole county. Not only that, but I have also seen them near my ranch. They have no business on the Zuni reservation. I know they were out here scouting my ranch, and now I'm missing some livestock. Damn, Navajos!" Strongbow roared.

"Calm down, Russ. Have you contacted the Zuni Police? That's their jurisdiction."

"I don't trust them. That's why I'm telling you this, Trefren. I know Jimmy is your cousin. Maybe you can get him to fess up against the other two, and I won't press charges against him, but I will against the other two punks."

"I'll admit, my cousin Jimmy will never win the *Citizen of the Year Award*, and Leaping Bear is about as dumb as they come, but Nate, he's a good kid with bad friends and a lot smarter than Jimmy or Chris. He's the only one of the three with a job. He delivers propane. He's been questioned for a few incidents but is clean."

"Maybe too smart to get caught, John. I hate those Navajos."

"I'll talk to my cousin, see what he knows, and speak with Nate. And remember this, Russell, I'm Navajo."

Strongbow had always been outspoken about his dislike of the Navajo people. "You're a Ramah Navajo, an outcast like me. That's why you and I have always gotten along," Strongbow said.

Dolly tapped her fingers on the table while waiting for Charlie to arrive. She noticed the two men sitting across the room as they laughed loudly. One was tall, dark, and muscular, with an opened shirt collar exposing his smooth chest. He liked his jewelry, Dolly thought. He wore a leather necklace with a single sizeable turquoise stone shaped like an arrowhead and a silver ring with multiple colored stones on almost every finger. The other man wore blue jeans, a Western sports jacket, and a navy blue Polo shirt. He was shorter than the muscular man and had a lighter complexion, but Native American and not as ornate and ostentatious as his friend.

Charlie walked into the restaurant past the two men and sat beside Dolly at the square dining table.

"That man is a police officer," Charlie said as he cocked his head toward the two men at the table.

"Which one?"

"The one that doesn't need all the attention. I saw the badge case he was wearing on his belt. Looks like he's got a gun under that coat, too."

"I bet you're starving, Charlie." She smiled.

"I'm going to order everything on the menu except for rabbit."

Dolly laughed. "Don't worry. I don't think they serve rabbit here."

Charlie leaned closer to Dolly. "What do you think we should do about the masks?" he asked in a hushed voice.

"I'm not sure. They're still claiming nothing has been taken from the Navajo Art Museum," Dolly said in almost a whisper.

"But don't you find it curious? Two men assault a security guard, enter the museum, and take nothing?"

"I'm sure the police are working on that now."

Charlie leaned back on his chair. "I'm going to find out. Come on, let's go to my room and order room service."

As they walked out, Charlie surprised Dolly when he approached the table with the two men.

"Sorry to bother you, but are you a police officer," he asked the man wearing the sports jacket.

"Yes, I'm Detective John Trefren with the Gallup Police Department," he said politely. "This is my friend Russell Strongbow, a resident from here."

Strongbow greeted them with a nod. He smiled at Dolly.

"I'm Chile Charlie, and this is Dolly Thompson. I was just wondering if they caught any suspects yet and if anything was stolen from the museum."

Strongbow's smile vanished, and they looked at Charlie with curiosity. "Why do you want to know," he asked.

"Just curious. I am interested in Native American culture, and Dolly here is an anthropologist."

"We're still working on the case," Detective Trefren informed them.

"Okay, thank you for your time," Charlie said looking directly at Trefren.

Charlie called for room service to his room. He ordered more food than he thought he could handle.

"You think we should let the police know about those masks?" Dolly asked.

Charlie had concerns about the valid owner of the Kachina masks. "They may not have come from the museum, Dolly. Let us wait."

"Then I think we should go and get those masks before someone else finds them, or worse yet, the person who hid them may return to get them, and we'll never see them again. But if we retrieve them, I'm sure someone will be troubled when they discover they're gone. Then we'll know who hid them there."

"That's what I'm afraid of," Charlie said.

◆◆◆◆◆◆◆◆◆◆

It was barely dusk when Chile Charlie parked the El Camino on the dirt trail where Magi Milly had dropped him off a few days before. Dolly wanted to go with him, but Charlie insisted there were too many dangers in that canyon, especially in the dark.

"It's best to wait here in the car," Charlie advised. "Tribal Police is patrolling the area, so keep the engine running, lights off, and don't step on the brakes, or you'll light up the desert, and they'll spot us from miles away."

"Are you sure you don't want me to come?" Dolly was a bit apprehensive about being left alone in the dark.

"You'll be okay. Keep the doors locked, and remember, my gun is in the glovebox with a round in the chamber and the safety off. It's ready to go. Just don't shoot until you're sure it's not me." Charlie disappeared into the darkness carrying a flashlight and his hiking stick.

He kept the flashlight down at a sharp angle, just enough to see in front of him. He walked along the base of the southern slope, where he knew he'd find the narrow gully. Charlie walked for nearly forty minutes before he found it. He turned the light off, stood motionless, and listened for any unusual noises, mostly humankind. He heard none. Charlie shined his flashlight up the slope and to the right until he spotted the juniper.

Dolly remained in the car, nervously alert. It seemed as if she had been waiting for hours. She heard a startling cracking noise from outside. Dolly couldn't see anything. She opened the glovebox and removed the .380 Beretta. She heard it again, approaching the passenger side of the car. She held the gun in both hands and pointed the muzzle toward the passenger window. Then, a light flashed on the ground and rapidly zigzagged in many directions. The light went up and shone on a man's face—it was Charlie. Dolly exhaled and realized she had been holding her breath.

Charlie kept the light on himself. "It's me, Dolly, don't shoot," he said as he approached the car. Charlie walked to the back of the car and unzipped his large suitcase. He removed all his clothes, placed the black sack into it, placed his clothing on top of the bag, and zipped up the suitcase.

♦♦♦♦♦♦♦♦♦♦

He took the masks from the black sack into Charlie's room and laid them across his bed.

"My God, Charlie. We are in trouble. These are actual Anasazi Kachina masks. These are worth the money. But who buried them in that canyon?"

"That's the whole mystery, Dolly."

"What are we going to do?"

"We're going to hide them, but first, I am taking pictures." Charlie took several photographs of the masks with his cell Phone. "I'm going to the public copier in the lobby and printing some copies. Wait here. I'll be right back." He left carrying his backpack and returned twenty minutes later.

Dolly was worried. She didn't expect that something like this would land on their laps. "I know a man at the University of New Mexico who's an expert in southwestern Native American culture. I think he can help us. His name is Dr. Levi Garcia.

"Don't you think he'll become suspicious, especially if he's an expert? He'll ask too many questions we don't want to answer."

"What's your plan, then?"

Charlie hesitated to answer. He didn't want to hurt her feelings, but it was necessary. "I can't tell you, Dolly. The less you know, the less you'll be in trouble if things go wrong."

Chapter Twelve

Evil Christmas Spirits

"Let's go open our Christmas present," Running Water quipped. He smiled anxiously like a little boy waiting for Santa Claus.

"Do you think the heat's off yet," Chris Leaping Bear asked?

"It's been two weeks now, and there's nothing new on the radio. I don't think they know about the missing masks. I think it's time." Jimmy said. "Go get the shovels and flashlights," he said as he searched for the key to his pickup truck.

Chris hurried to do as Jimmy ordered.

"Don't forget the whiskey. And hurry. I don't want to waste any more time here. We're going to be rich!" Running Water exclaimed.

It was a moonless night as the boys drove back to the canyon. They were in merry spirits with laughter and song. They hadn't drunk yet. The whiskey was for celebration after the retrieval of their treasure. The boys sang "Jingle Bells" at the top of their lungs until they arrived at the canyon.

The site was more challenging to find than the merry boys thought. They scanned slowly with flashlights, searching for over an hour in the cold. They finally found the large juniper tree and the two large rocks. Jimmy noticed that the two rocks appeared to have been moved. No coyote could have moved them, he thought. Worry set in, then anger, and then fear. Someone knows we've been here, he thought.

Leaping Bear dug and dug while Running Water held the flashlights. He reached the bottom of the hole — no sack. That was Jimmy's fear.

"What happened to our treasure?" Leaping Bear shouted, "Somebody stole our masks!"

Running Water remained silent, looking down into the hole. His eyes burned with anger as his mind dug for answers.

"What are we going to do? Those masks belong to us, Jimmy. We've got to find them!" Leaping Bear exclaimed.

"Shut up and let me think!" There was silence. Running Water thought. "Let's go pay a visit to the medicine woman. She knows everything that goes on in the canyon. I bet she knows who's been out here, and I bet she knows about the masks too . . . I know she does."

"We can't do that tonight. It's too late, and we don't want to upset her," Leaping Bear said. "Let's go back to Gallup and come back in the morning to see Milly," he suggested.

They drove in poor spirits, this time without song. It was a silent night.

Jimmy and Chris were up and ready to go in the dark morning. Though they were tired from the long drive home, neither had a restful night. Jimmy spent the night thinking about all the trouble they had gone through—the museum, the burial of the masks, the retrieval, and now, they wake up empty-handed in Gallup, New Mexico.

"It is too early to go see Milly," Chris said. He feared upsetting the old woman.

"No, it's not. That witch never sleeps, and I want to get those masks back before it's too late." Jimmy said with anger. They were in trouble. The meeting with the buyer was taking place that afternoon.

◆◆◆◆◆◆◆◆◆◆

Milly walked outside to the cool, fresh desert air and sat on her rocking chair every morning. The light began to glow behind the mountains on the eastern horizon. She sat motionless and listened to the desert, wrapped in an old wool blanket of faded earth colors. Her excellent great-grandmother had woven that blanket back when the Navajo fought to preserve their freedom. It was passed on to Milly only to fight against the cold.

The sun rose above the horizon, and the silence was broken by the sound of an approaching truck that could be heard in the distance. She recognized that sound.

"Good morning, Milly," Running Water said as he exited the truck. "Is Nate here?"

"No, he left for town again," Milly said.

By the scowl on her face, Jimmy knew she was already upset. "Do you have time to talk to us? We want to ask you a few questions."

"It depends on the questions," Milly answered.

"Have you noticed any strange people coming around the canyon lately, maybe tourists or hikers?"

Milly noticed Leaping Bear sitting in the truck, and it appeared he was not getting out. "I know the spirits in the canyon have been disturbed." She glanced back at Running Water. "Why do you ask?" Milly said with cynical eyes. "Did you lose something out there?"

"No reason in particular; we were just curious. We thought that we could get jobs as guides." Does she know what we've been doing down there? Running Water wondered. "We just wanted to know if there's been anyone out there, you know, to help them in case they got lost," he said.

"The Spirits tell me that only noisy demons have been down there. Maybe they have sent the *spirit coyote* to expel the demons from the canyon," she said.

Running Water didn't know what to make of that. "Bueno, we'll leave you in peace to watch the sun do its thing or whatever you do," he said disrespectfully. He turned and looked about at Milly's place as if he was looking for something or perhaps scheming.

"What are you looking for?" Milly asked as she pushed the blanket away in front of her. "I told you Young Owl is not here."

Jimmy froze, staring at a .45 Colt revolver in an old, worn-out, brown leather cross-draw holster on Milly's belt. She's old, maybe too weak to lift the gun or pull the trigger, Jimmy thought, but this was not a good time to find out. Without another word, he turned slowly and got into the pickup truck. They drove away, leaving a cloud of red dust that could be seen for several miles.

"What did Milly tell you?" Leaping Bear asked.

"Nothing! It's just her crazy talk about spirits. That old witch!" Jimmy didn't mention Milly's revolver. He pounded the steering wheel with his fist. "Our buyer is coming to Gallup today. We gotta find those masks soon." Jimmy understood the severity of their situation if they were to show up at the meeting empty-handed.

"What are we going to do now," Chris asked.

Jimmy had thought about tying the old woman and searching the entire place for the black sack, but the rumor about Milly was confirmed: she did carry a gun. As far back as Jimmy could remember, there were stories about the old medicine woman and how deadly she was with a six-shooter. It was said that Magi Milly once shot and killed a man for trying to steal her sheep. She buried him in the desert; the body was never found, but that was only a rumor. When Nate moved in with his grandmother, the other children asked him if the stories about Milly were true. Nate neither confirmed nor denied the rumors.

Jimmy was becoming desperate. "She knows something but won't talk, but I know someone who will."

◆◆◆◆◆◆◆◆◆◆

Nate Greystone drove Milly's truck to the village of Crystal to pick up the propane truck for an early morning service at one of the remote ranches. Cell phone reception was better in Crystal, and Nate could read all the messages. One of the text messages read:

Meet me by the entrance at the airport.

After he did the propane service, Nate returned the propane truck to the company yard and headed south for the airport near Gallup in Milly's truck.

Chapter Thirteen

Land of the People

It was midmorning when Charlie arrived at Milly's house. He noticed her pickup truck was not there and wondered if anyone was home. He stepped out of his truck anyway.

Milly appeared at the door. "Chile Charlie, I saw you in my dream that you would come here today to tell me something important." She motioned him to enter.

Charlie walked in with his backpack and placed it on the table. "Good morning, Milly."

"You want some coffee to wake your spirit?"

Charlie gave her a single nod.

"What troubles you, Chile Charlie?

"I have something I want to show you." He reached into the backpack, took out several sheets of paper, and handed them to Milly.

She studied the photos briefly, then placed them on the table and sat down. Milly lit her pipe and blew the smoke up, creating a hazy cloud.

"The ancients were the farming tribes who lived in the dwellings of the mountains." She pointed to the pictures.

"These are the masks of the Kachinas. They were benevolent beings from the underworld. They appeared before the ancients and danced to make rain for their crops. But the enemy of the ancients killed the Kachinas, and their spirits were sent to dwell at the bottom of the desert lake for eternity, but they left the masks, in their image, in the desert for the people to find. The Spirit of the Kachinas is in the masks, and those who wear them will become the embodiment of the Kachinas, and they too can make rain."

Milly looked hard into Charlie's eyes. "Where did you find these pictures, Chile Charlie?

He hesitated to say, but her stare was too intense. She may already know the truth, he thought. Charlie told her how he found the black sack buried in the canyon.

"What will you do with them," Milly asked.

"Well, there are no reports of missing Kachina masks from the break-in of the museum in Gallup, and there aren't any claims from the owner anywhere in the news or the internet. I'd hate for them to end up in the wrong hands."

"Those masks belong to the desert, not in a museum . . ."

"And not in the federal government archives," Charlie inserted.

"Charlie, I am worried about Young Owl. He's gone again. I rode my horse out this morning after sunrise, and when I returned, he was gone. He left me a note that he was going into Crystal for a propane service and would then return." She took a small blue piece of paper out of the pocket of her wool sweater and placed it on the table."

"May I see that," Charlie asked.

Milly pushed the note to Charlie. He unfolded the note and read it."

"Where do you think he went?"

"He likes to go visit with his friends with bad spirits. He goes to a house called Blackrock. It is just an old house belonging to Sam Blackrock. It's a hideaway in the hills south of Gallup, maybe five or seven miles. Not a good place."

"I'll go look for him." Charlie reached to take the photos, but Milly grabbed them quickly. She went to the iron cooking stove, opened the firebox door, and threw the sheets of paper into the burning wood. "These were not meant for one to see," she said.

Charlie looked at her blankly for a moment, then nodded in agreement.

"Be careful, Chile Charlie. There is nothing there but black hearts. Charlie left and sat in his El Camino for a moment. He watched Milly walk behind the house toward the stable.

Chapter Fourteen

Perea Corrals

Stephan Giles rode comfortably in the back seat of a black Chevy Suburban. It wasn't the trip from Albuquerque International Airport that bothered him. It was the desolate land of the truck stop, red hills, lava rock, semi-trucks, and wide open space of nothingness. It was unlike Dallas, Texas, where he came in the company jet.

He carried a tan, hard leather travel bag, hand-tooled with the circle star, long horns, the Texas flag, and barbed wire patterns that made it look like a fancy saddlebag. The travel bag was pure Texas, and it held oil money.

Giles dressed like a Texan with a charcoal gray western suit, a white dress shirt with a bolo tie, a shiny silver belt buckle, and polished black boots. He had reddish-blonde hair under a black Stetson hat, and mysterious eyes were hidden behind a pair of Oakleys. He was the runner for his boss, a millionaire oil man, buyer, and collector of rare southwestern antiquities obtained illegally. He was accompanied by his assistant and driver, Simon, a six-foot, two-inch tall ex-Texas Ranger.

The Suburban arrived at *Perea*, a place with a name but no town; only the *Iyanbito* Gospel Lighthouse Church was there. Simon traveled north on the freeway to an isolated dirt road that led to the abandoned corrals, where they parked and waited.

Stephan patted the tan leather bag resting next to him. It contained $500,000 in one-hundred-dollar bills. "Simon, when he arrives, get out and just stand by the door," he told his driver. There was no drawl to his voice, more upper Midwest than Texan.

Five minutes later, a white KIA SUV arrived and stopped about thirty feet away, facing the front of the black Suburban. The driver and passenger doors opened simultaneously. The driver exited the vehicle.

Giles exited his vehicle and left the leather bag in the back seat. He motioned the driver of the KIA to step closer. They met in the middle between the two facing cars.

"Hello, Mr. Giles. Good to see you again."

"Hello, Lee. Do you have the goods?"

"They will be here shortly."

Although the notion of going home with half a million dollars excited him, Lee's nervous voice betrayed him. He had not heard from Jimmy Running Water, who had also not answered the multiple calls made to his phone.

"You mean, you arrived here without the merchandise?" Mr. Giles said.

"I can assure you, the carrier will arrive here shortly," Lee explained.

"Lee, I'm a patient man, so I'll give your carrier twenty minutes, and that's all."

Mr. Giles returned to the suburban and sat in the back seat. "Simon, when I get out of the car, make the call."

Lee returned to his KIA and slammed the door. "Call Jimmy again and find out where the hell he is," he told his passenger.

Twenty minutes passed, and the masks did not arrive.

"Lee, are you playing me?"

"No, Mr. Giles. We don't know what happened to the man supposed to meet us here."

Stephan Giles puts his arm around Lee's shoulders as if they were pals. "Lee, we've done business together many times in the past. This is the first time you've disappointed us."

"But Mr. Giles, you don't understand . . ."

"I understand that you have lost control here." He glanced at Lee's SUV. "And you brought some muscle with you?"

"You've brought muscle too, Mr. Giles," Lee said with a subtle tone of insolence.

"I've got five hundred thousand dollars to protect. You have nothing." Mr. Giles said emphatically. He turned to look at his driver.

Simon shook his head with subtle motions.

"I'm sorry, Lee. I'm afraid we will no longer require your services. Please take us off your contact list."

Stephan Giles turned sharply to return to the black Suburban.

"Wait! Mr. Giles, I can get those masks to you," Lee shouted.

The black suburban sped away and covered Lee in a cloud of dust. Lee returned to his white SUV.

"I want you to find this Jimmy Running Water," Lee said furiously. "Get the masks back. And take care of him. I don't care what you do. Do you get me?" Lee said, pointing his finger at his passenger.

"I get you, Lee, but it's not just Jimmy I have to take care of. There are two others, and that will cost you extra," Russell Strongbow said.

Chapter Fifteen

Braided Tail

Nate Greystone arrived at Blackrock and parked next to Jimmy Running Water's truck. It was quiet except for the closing of the driver's door. Too early for these bums to be up, Nate thought. The front door flew open before he reached the three steps to the porch deck. Jimmy walked out with Chris trailing behind.

"Where've you been? Jimmy shouted.

"I've been looking for you all morning," Nate said as he reached into his outer coat pocket. "I have a message for you." He handed the note to Jimmy.

Jimmy yanked the blue paper out of Nate's hand and read the message.

Iyanbito church, n .3 mi, left .2 mi to Perea corrales, 1pm

"A bit too late." Jimmy crumbled the note and tossed it in the front seat of his truck through the opened passenger window. "We've been looking for you too."

He grabs Greystones by the coat and pulls him in close. "Okay, shrimp, I want to know where my masks are, or I will tear your limbs from your body."

"What masks? I don't even know what you're talking about."

"You know what I'm talking about, the sack with the four Kachina masks," Jimmy said.

"The ones you stole from us from the canyon!" Chris Leaking Bear shouted from the porch.

"We know you took the sack, and I want it back now!" Jimmy demanded.

Nate grabbed Jimmy's wrists and shoved him back. "I don't have your damn masks. I didn't take them."

"Well, if you didn't take them, then only one other person could have taken them, your grandmother. She told us that she knew we'd been in the canyon."

Nate began to worry. "When did she tell you that?"

"We visited her this morning when we looked for you. Maybe we'll go back and visit the old witch, only this time she'll give us our masks, or I will take her scalp. That should be worth some money."

Jimmy had never called Milly an 'old witch,' and it infuriated Nate that his friend threatened to harm his grandmother. He cocked his right hand back and struck Jimmy on the left side of his face with a punch that sent him flying onto the porch steps.

"If you ever come near our house again, I will kill you and bury you in the desert where no one will ever find you." Nate knew he had a tough fight coming. Jimmy was slightly taller, broader, and stronger.

Jimmy got up slowly. "Greystone, maybe we should call you *Yellowstone* instead. You were always a coward. You never got caught, and we were the ones who always went to jail."

"That's because you're stupid, along with your yellow dog here." He pointed at Chris.

Jimmy pulled a knife with a seven-and-a-half-inch blade from the leather sheath on his belt. "Big words from a little man," Jimmy said.

Nate removed his coat, threw it on the ground, reached behind him, and drew his Bowie knife with the fourteen-inch blade. "Big knife for a big man," Nate responded.

Jimmy's eyes widened, and Leaping Bear's jaw dropped open. Neither of them had seen that knife before, just as they had never seen the medicine bag Nate had always carried.

"Don't think about it, Jimmy," Nate warned. "My grandfather was the best knife fighter on the reservation. I carry his blood, and you're not that good."

"Teach him a lesson, Jimmy!" Chris shouted from the porch, careful to keep his distance from the knives.

Jimmy approached Nate, crouched with feigning movements. Nate remained calm, holding his knife in his right hand with the blunt side down. Jimmy lunged at Nate for a stab to the stomach. With the Bowie knife's blunt side, Nate struck Jimmy's wrist and instantly swung the blade up and across Jimmy's upper chest, cutting his plaid shirt and black-hooded jacket. Jimmy felt an instant stream of current numbing rush up his arm, almost making him drop his knife. He stepped back and looked at his chest—no blood.

Jimmy charged Nate with wild, slashing swings. Nate avoided the sharp blade with dodges and shifting movements without overreacting. Jimmy swung for a cross slash. In two quick moves, Nat struck the wrist with the blunt end again and turned back across Jimmy's face while simultaneously grappling the knife-wielding wrist. It was only a surface cut to the right side of the face. Jimmy dropped the knife as he stepped away from his opponent. Nate kicked Jimmy's groin with the force of a wild Mustang. Jimmy bowed over on his knees. Nate walked behind him and kicked his back, sending Jimmy's face to the ground.

Nate straddled Jimmy's back. "I'm not going to kill you, but I am taking your scalp. You don't deserve to go to the spirit world. With his left hand, Nate grabbed a hand full of hair. He yanked the head back and placed the sharp blade at the top of the forehead.

"Nate, Don't do it!" Chris Leaping Bear yelled.

Nate closed his eyes, tilted his head back, gave out Indian whoops, and shouted, *"Nílch'i!"* With one quick movement, Nate made a slashing cut. "I will hang this in my hogan," Nate declared as he held the long braided ponytail up.

Jimmy moaned as he came back to a higher level of consciousness.

"Waste Water. The next time you show up to my house, I will have my grandmother put a spell on you, and you'll be crapping horned toads for the rest of your wasted life . . . and that's going to hurt every time.

Nate picked up Jimmy's knife and walked to the porch, where Chris squatted with teary eyes. "Where's your knife?"

"I don't have one," Chris said shakenly.

Nate dropped Jimmy's knife in front of the frightened boy. "Here, this is yours now. Maybe you'll be wiser with it. Nate walked down the steps, stopped, and turned.

"You know, Chris. Just because you raise sheep doesn't mean you have to be one. Become a mountain lion, and I'll stop calling you *Leaking* Bear." Nate took the braided ponytail and placed it in his medicine bag.

◆◆◆◆◆◆◆◆◆◆

Dolly was about to finish her coffee when she saw Nate Greystone enter the hotel lobby. She left her table to greet him. "Nate, what are you doing here?"

He was caught by surprise. "I'm looking for Charlie."

"He's not here right now."

Dolly thought Nate looked like he'd been in a fight. "He won't be here for a while, but if you want to wait for him, I'll buy you breakfast or lunch. Come on."

Dolly noticed the concerned look on the boy's face. She saw him as a boy, but he wasn't. He was built like a man, about five nine, with a slender body and broad shoulders, indicating he was a hard physical worker. He had large brown eyes under the prominent superciliary arches and smooth skin on his oval face.

Perhaps it was the look on his face, an innocence behind those angry eyes. His long hair was split in the center and pulled back in a ponytail. He wore tan canvas pants and a black pullover wool sweater under a faded olive drab army field jacket. It was as if he tried not to look Native American.

"How did you know to find Charlie here," Dolly asked.

"I saw his cream and turquoise colored truck parked in the parking lot a few days ago. I just figured he stays here."

Dolly told him about her background and why she was in Gallup. She was curious about this troubled young man. "What's it like living here in Gallup?"

"I didn't grow up here. My parents sent me here to live with my grandparents." He cast his eyes down almost in shame, admitting he was unwanted by his family. "They thought the demon spirits possessed me. They figured my grandmother could heal me. I've only been here seven years."

"Did it work? Did your grandmother heal you?"

"Dolly, I don't have evil spirits in me. I grew up being a little troublemaker and a criminal when I was still a juvenile, but all that stopped when I moved here. It's just that my reputation followed me here. I graduated from high school and have a job delivering propane to ranches and houses outside the city. The only demon I have is my reputation."

"Have you been in trouble here?"

"No, but the sheriff, the tribal police, and the Gallup Police Department have questioned me many times, primarily because of my only two friends. They're the criminals. He began to feel that he trusted Dolly and talked openly to her.

"When I first moved here, the kids teased me because of my grandmother. They called her a witch and a crazy woman, even though she's a tribal Shaman. But many rumors about my grandmother existed long before I came here."

"You've only had two friends all this time?"

Jimmy Running Water and Chris Leaping Bear were the only kids who didn't make fun of me. I call Jimmy 'Waste Water' because he's dirty. He fights dirty, and he steals from his people. Chris is not so bright and follows Jimmy like a trained dog. I call him 'Leaking Bear' because he acts like he pees his pants every time Jimmy gives him an order."

"Why do you hang around with boys like that?"

"I don't anymore. Things changed after high school. Jimmy and Chris have worsened, but I occasionally see them at Blackrock's. It's an abandoned house converted into a bar where everyone parties. I discovered the place when I first started delivering propane. I stay there sometimes when I'm in town. That's why I wanted to see Mr. Chile Charlie."

"I don't understand."

"I think they're the ones who broke into the museum."

"But the radio said nothing was taken," she reminded him.

"That's where everyone is wrong. Four rare Kachina masks were taken."

◆◆◆◆◆◆◆◆◆◆

Chris Leaping Bear drove alone into town in Jimmy's truck to get lunch back to Blackwater. The Nearest Taco Bell was on Historic 60. After going through the drive-thru, Chris drove to gas up at a service station on the next block on the west end of the El Rancho Hotel front parking lot. He was about to leave when Nate came out of the hotel and walked toward Milly's truck.

As Nate backed up to leave, Chris drove behind him and honked his horn to get his attention. Nate exited his vehicle, ready to deal with Jimmy again, but realized it was only Chris.

"Nate, hey, I'm sorry about all that with Jimmy. It's just that the buyer for the Kachina masks was here today, and we missed the meeting. That was $10,000 for each of us. That's why he was so angry. He thought you or your grandmother took the black sack we hid in the canyon."

"I didn't know anything about those masks until today," Nate told him.

"Anyway. I wanted to warn you about Strongbow. He's in this too and probably wants to talk to you."

"I know about Russell Strongbow. He's the one who asked me if I knew anyone for a job, but I didn't know what the job was going to be. He just told me I would receive a finder's fee." That note I gave Jimmy was from Strongbow."

"I thought you were the messenger."

"No, I just gave Jimmy a lead on a job. That's all."

Chapter Sixteen

Bad Day at Blackrock

Sam Blackrock sat behind the ill-constructed bar reading a magazine when Russell Strongbow bolted into the house like a raging grizzly bear.

"Where are they, Sam? He shouted.

Where's who?"

"Running Water and Leaping Bear, that's who!"

Chris isn't here, but Jimmy's in the back," Sam said, pointing to the hallway. "He's had a rough day already."

"It's gonna get a lot rougher," Strongbow said.

Strongbow kicked the door open and found Jimmy lying on a cot. He rushed towards Jimmy, lifted him by his shirt, and threw him against the wall. "Why didn't you show up at the meeting when you were supposed to?" He didn't give Jimmy a chance to answer. He grabbed him by the shirt again and pushed his face to the floor.

Jimmy was tough, but Strongbow was too powerful, too crazy, and too unpredictable. "Wait, Russ, I can explain!"

As Jimmy pushed himself up, Russell kicked his upper chest with a force that flipped Jimmy over on his back. "You're stealing the masks for yourselves, aren't you?"

"No! I'm telling you the truth. We weren't trying to steal them. Someone else stole them from us."

"What are you talking about?"

"We hid them in the canyon, and someone else dug them up when we returned."

"You expect me to believe a cheap lying thief like you?" Russell lifted Jimmy from the floor and was about to punch him.

"No! Wait! It's true. I think I know who has the masks. It's Nate Greystone and his grandmother."

"You mean Magi Milly?"

"Yes, we went to see her, and she knew we had been in the canyon. It had to be her and Greystone."

"I should have suspected that," Strongbow said, "Greystone's a lot smarter than you and Squatting Bear. Where's Greystone now?"

"He's on his way home. He came here to give us the message about the meeting."

Russell notices the recent cut on Jimmy's face and the blunt haircut on the right side of his head. He realized the braided ponytail was gone. "He did that to you?"

Jimmy nodded. "Nate was angry because we went to see his grandmother."

"Did you search her house?"

"No."

Why not?"

Jimmy didn't respond.

Strongbow shook him. "Why Not!"

"She pulled a gun on us. That's why!"

Russell Strongbow chuckled. "Stay here. When your boyfriend, Stupid Bear, shows up, tell him to stay put, don't leave. Russell opened the left side of his brown leather vest to reveal a concealed handgun in a leather shoulder holster.

"When I pull a gun, I use it." I'll be back later.

"Where are you going?" Jimmy asked.

"I'm not afraid of an old Medicine woman with a gun."

◆◆◆◆◆◆◆◆◆

Charlie took the Miyamura exit from I-40 and headed south towards the hotel to pick up Dolly. He stopped for the red light at Ford Drive and Historic 60. The El Rancho Hotel was located on the southwest corner of the intersection. He glanced at the hotel and saw Milly's truck in the parking lot facing west and another truck parked directly behind. Neither truck was parked in a parking stall.

The traffic light turned green, and Charlie decided to continue south on Ford Drive for a better view. He saw Nate talking with another man, and they seemed to be having a serious discussion. Charlie continued south, turned left on Aztec Avenue, and immediately turned right onto the rear entrance of the hotel's east parking lot. He drove slowly into the parking lot, just far enough to get a distant view of the two boys. Something did not look right, Chile Charlie thought.

Dolly was about to watch TV when her cell phone rang.

"Dolly, we must go. Leave by the rear hotel entrance and wait for me on the street. Call me when you're there."

"Charlie, you're scaring me. What's going on?

"I'll explain when I pick you up. Hurry!"

Charlie hung up intentionally to avoid further questions from Dolly. He kept an eye on Nate and the other man. He took out the note that Nate had left for his grandmother. It's the same notepad paper, and the writing looks the same, Charlie thought. His cell phone rang. It was Dolly.

"Charlie, I'm here now."

Charlie slowly backed his El Camino, turned around, and exited the same entrance he drove into. He stopped on the road at the back of the hotel where Dolly waited.

"Hurry, get in! Something's going on in the front of the hotel with Nate. He's talking to some guy," he explained.

Charlie drives north onto Navajo Drive and heads towards Historic 60, then turns right into the back of a convenience store at the west end of the hotel parking lot. He stopped. From there, he had a good view of the boys.

"Nate came into the hotel looking for you," Dolly told him.

"He left the hotel some time ago. I didn't know he was still here."

They watched Nate and the other man jumped into their trucks. Nate left the parking lot first, heading west on Historic 60. The other truck followed directly behind. As they passed by, Charlie and Dolly heard the roar of the second truck. Charlie backed up onto Navajo Drive and followed the trucks. He kept his distance so as not to be noticed.

"What's wrong, Charlie? You look serious?" she said.

"Greystone is involved in something, but I don't know for sure." He handed Dolly the blue note. "It's the same size, type, and color as the one I found in your room. Not only that, I recognized the sound of that truck following Nate. It's the same one I heard the night I searched your room and the one we heard that night in Tohatchi."

It suddenly dawned on Dolly. "Charlie!" she shouted.

"What?"

"Waste water," she said excitedly. "Nate told me that one of the boys he hangs around with is named Running Water. Nate calls him 'Waste Water.' The note was for his friend."

"Damn! That means Nate is involved." He paused. "You better call Gallup P.D. and get a hold of that Detective Trefren. Let him know what's going on, but don't mention anything about Kachina masks." Charlie paused. "That also means Nate knows who your boy is."

"What, Boy?" Dolly asked, surprised.

"You know . . . the one who attempted to rob you."

◆◆◆◆◆◆◆◆◆◆

Chile Charlie and Dolly followed the two trucks. Nate continued west, and Chris Leaping Bear turned south on Second Street. Charlie followed the loud truck.

"I think he's heading for a place called Blackrock," Dolly said. "Nate said it was about seven miles south of Gallup."

Charlie continued south until the road changed to NM 602. He kept his distance. They had been out of the city for several miles and were now in open country of sage-covered hills. "Look, he's turning left onto that dirt road," he said.

The loud truck sped up, leaving a trail of dust. Charlie followed. He couldn't see the truck but could hear the noisy, out-of-tune engine. He followed the dust trail for about a mile until it turned left onto a side road that sloped up a hill. Below the opposite side of the hill was a small valley of about five acres of flat desert land.

A white stucco house stood in the center of the valley, hidden among the hills.

"That must be Blackrock," Dolly said.

The noisy truck was parked in front of the house with no driver. Chris had walked into the house carrying a bag of tacos and a cardboard tray with two large soft drinks. As he entered the room, Jimmy jumped up from the cot.

"What took you so long? We gotta leave here now and hide somewhere as far as possible! Strongbow was here, and he thinks we stole the masks. I know he means to kill us."

"Where is he now?" Chris said, frightened.

"I told him about Nate and his grandmother. He's headed there now. If they have those Kachina masks, Strongbow will find them."

"If he finds them, why do we have to hide?" Chris asked.

"Just in case he doesn't find them."

They rushed out of the room and headed for the front door. When they reached the porch, they saw Charlie standing next to Jimmy's truck and Dolly standing next to Charlie's El Camino.

"So, you're the man with the El Camino. What are you doing here," Jimmy asked.

He had previously seen Charlie's vehicle in the hotel parking lot—a cream and turquoise 1959 El Camino was easy to spot anywhere.

"I'm here to ask a few questions. Are you Running Water?"

"Why do you want to know?"

"Because Nate Greystone is our friend, and I think he's involved in some kind of illegal activity with you two bums."

Jimmy walked down the porch steps towards his truck past Charlie. "I don't have time to answer questions, especially to a white man."

Charlie grabbed Jimmy by his coat, spun him around, and slammed him onto the driver's door. Dolly pulled open the front of her coat and revealed her holster with a revolver.

Chris dropped the tray of drinks. "Jimmy, she's got a gun!" he shouted.

"Make time, punk," Charlie said to Jimmy.

"I'll tell you what to want to know, mister!" Chris shouted. "Nate is our friend. We think he stole something from us."

"Like what, Kachina masks?" Charlie said.

The boys were stunned.

"Was Nate involved in that museum break-in?" Charlie asked.

"No, he had nothing to do with it," Chris said.

"Shut up, Chris! Jimmy shouted.

"I don't care about the museum. As far as anybody knows, nothing was taken. All you're responsible for is forced entry and putting a guard to sleep," Charlie explained.

Charlie looked at Dolly.

She nodded. She recognized the man who attempted to rob her.

Charlie noticed an old scar on the left side of Jimmy's face. "By the way, Mr. Running Water, does my friend look familiar to you?"

Jimmy looked at Dolly and didn't respond.

"This is for Dolly," Charlie swung his right fist forward and slammed it into Jimmy's face. Jimmy's legs buckled, and his body slowly slid against the driver's door.

"Don't go anywhere," Charlie said to Chris. There's a man on his way right now. His name is Detective John Trefren. He'll have questions for the both of you."

Charlie was about to walk away when he noticed a crumpled blue notepad paper on the seat of Jimmy's truck. He reached through the open window, took it out, and read it. He waved the blue note at Chris. "You don't mind if I take this, do you," he asked.

"No, take it," Chris said. "There's something you need to know. There's another man involved. His name is Russell Strongbow. He was here and roughed up Jimmy.

"He thinks Nate's grandmother might have those masks. He's *muy malo*, a bad man.

"So what?"

"He's gone to see Magi Milly . . . he'll kill her and Greystone.

◆◆◆◆◆◆◆◆◆◆

Nate headed to the Gallup Police Department to speak with Detective Trefren. It was time to let him know everything. He was willing to go to jail for his part, and he was done with Blackrock and his two friends, who turned out not to be true friends.

Trefren was away from his office. He had been out investigating an armed robbery of a liquor store that had taken place the previous night.

Nate decided to pick up his paycheck from the Arco Propane Company, get something to eat, and then head home to speak with his grandmother. He planned to tell her about his involvement with Jimmy and Chris and the stolen and missing Sacred Kachina masks. As a Shaman, she would be most interested to know.

Chapter Seventeen

Black Heart

Nate placed his hand on his medicine bag as he drove home. It was time to take his culture seriously. The handle of the Bowie irritated his back, and he slipped it from inside his belt and placed it beside him on the bench seat.

When he arrived home, he saw Strongbow's Dodge Ram parked in front of the hogan. *"What the hell is he doing here,"* Nate wondered. Maybe he wants me to give Jimmy another message, or he's looking for those two idiots.

Nate noticed that Milly's horse was missing from the stable. He walked into the house and found it in complete disarray. The place had been ransacked. The table had been turned over, and everything in the dresser drawers and nightstands had been thrown on the floor.

"Surprised to find me here?" Russell Strongbow stood just outside the door.

"Why did you do this? You're looking for those masks, aren't you?"

"Where are they? Your friends seemed to think that you have them."

"They're not my friends anymore, and I don't have your masks. Where's my grandmother?"

"Tell me where the Kachina masks are, and I'll tell you where I have her hidden."

Anger rose in Greystone. "I told you; I don't have them, and if you've hurt my grandmother, I promise I will kill you."

Strongbow gave a fake laugh. "That seems to run in the family. But you won't kill me. Not when I have this." Strongbow pulled the .9mm Glock from his shoulder holster under his brown leather vest and pointed it at Nate's face.

Strongbow heard the approaching car. He instinctively turns his head. Nate grabs the gun and punches Strongbow in the face simultaneously. Strongbow attempts to loosen Nate's grip without success. He repeatedly hit Nate on the right side of his face until he released his grip. Strongbow's instinct was to shoot Nate, but not with a car approaching. He struck Nate's left side of the face with the side of the gun. Nate stumbled but still reached to grab the gun. Three more strikes to the face with the side of the weapon, and Nate fell unconscious.

Charlie's El Camino came to a sliding halt near the hogan. He rushed out of the car, and before he reached the front door, Strongbow came out of the hogan, pointing his gun at Charlie.

"Stop right there! Strongbow shouted. "Put your hands up where I can see them."

"No, you drop the gun and put your hands up where I can see them," Dolly shouted.

When he rushed out the door, Russell was so focused on dealing with Charlie that he failed to see Dolly standing behind him.

Strongbow looked to his left and saw a black woman pointing a .38 revolver directly at him. A flashing thought of Milly entered his mind. Had she summoned these demons to take me away? Reality came back. Federal Agents, he thought. Strongbow did not move or drop the gun. When he heard the hammer clicking as Dolly thumbed it back, he tossed his Glock to his right.

Charlie approached closer and bent over to pick up the gun. The force of Strongbow's kick on his upper chest flipped Charlie onto his back. The Glock flew out of his hands behind him. Strongbow dashed to pick it up, but Charlie rose, charged, and stuck Strongbow on his upper chest with his left shoulder and drove him back as if he was protecting the quarterback from a charging linebacker. They both crashed against the hogan. Charlie stepped back.

Dolly hesitated to shoot an unarmed man, but she resolved to shoot if the Strongbow was to pick up the gun.

The two men moved and weaved about, taking a measure of each other. They were of equal size, but Strongbow outweighed Chile Charlie with pure muscle and hatred. Strongbow whipped out his dagger from the sheath and lunged forward. Chile Charlie's hand met the descending blade with a claw-like grip of the wrist as his right fist crashed into Strongbow's face with all the power he could muster. The staggering blow took Strongbow by complete surprise. Before he could regain his balance, Chile Charlie drove another full-force punch into Strongbow's mouth as he held on to the wrist. The knife fell from Strongbow's hand.

Dazed and disarmed, Strongbow struck wildly and blindly. He had not expected this lanky man to hit so hard and quickly. Charlie continued to shoot stunning blows into Strongbow's bloody face. He knew he had gained the advantage and would not take any risks. Both men paused, breathing hard, covered with blood from the splatter of the punches. Strongbow was blinded with blood and battered with a broken nose. He yielded ground, staggered back, then charged forward. Charlie swung his right fist, but Strongbow ducked and caught Charlie's left jaw with an agonizing right hook punch from the powerful man. Charlie fell back, dazed.

Strongbow turned and picked up his gun, but Charlie pounced on him like a mountain lion. The gun fired a single round as they struggled to control the weapon. Charlie heard a shrill cry. He saw Dolly drop to the ground but didn't see Strongbow's fist as it came down on his face. He staggered back, then saw the .9mm Glock pointed at him again.

"You'll die for this," Strongbow shouted through swollen lips. He lifted the gun to take careful aim at Charlie's head.

So, this is where it ends for Chile Charlie, Charlie thought sadly, but not for himself. He was thinking about Dolly, lying lifeless in a pool of blood. With teary eyes, he looked squarely at the man about to take his life. The fire of the shot echoed loudly throughout the valley and instantly made Charlie's body flinch with a tremble.

Strongbow fell to his knees, bewildered. His left arm dangled with excruciating pain. The elbow bled. He looked up and saw the woman on a horse with a .45 revolver in her hand.

"Magi Milly," Strongbow said. He lifted his Glock to shoot the old woman.

The second shot went through his right thigh. Strongbow fell over, still holding on to his handgun.

"The third shot will be going right through your black heart, Russell Strongbow, and I will bury you in the desert where you will never be found," Milly warned.

The muscular man with the jewelry dropped the gun. Charlie was still as he watched this scene take place. It was surreal—like one of those Western movies he loves to watch.

Charlie picked up Strongbow's gun and knife and ran over to Dolly. She moaned with pain. The .9mm bullet had struck her on the left leg through the femoral artery. Charlie removed his shirt, cut it with Strongbow's knife, and made a tourniquet to stop the bleeding. Milly went inside the hogan, where Greystone was lying on the floor, bleeding from the face but conscious.

Charlie noticed the CB antenna on the Dodge Ram. He called for help on the emergency channel and requested medical assistance for two shooting victims and an injured victim. He carried Dolly onto Milly's bed. With reluctance, he attended to Strongbow's injuries and stabilized him until the ambulance arrived. Charlie left him on the ground, agonized from the bullet wounds.

♦♦♦♦♦♦♦♦♦♦

John Trefren arrived in his unmarked police car, lights flashing and siren blaring. He jumped out of his car with a gun as he assessed the crime scene. He saw Charlie come out of the hogan.

"How did you get here so soon," Charlie asked.

"Chris Leaping Bear told me there would be trouble here. I was just a few miles away when the emergency call came out on the police radio." Trefren smiled. The Calvary is on its way."

Within the hour, many emergency units were on the scene—the tribal police, sheriff's department, fire department, ambulances, two medical helicopters, and the FBI.

Strongbow was flown out in one medical helicopter, handcuffed to the gurney. Dolly was flown in the other medical chopper, and Greystone was transported by ambulance. Everyone was taken to Gallup Indian Medical Center, where Dolly underwent immediate surgery. It was late evening when all the police investigations, scene processing, and interviews were concluded.

Charlie headed for the hospital to see Dolly. The hospital receptionist informed him that Dolly was recovering in the ICU.

Dolly was asleep, connected to monitors and IV. The attending nurse checked her vitals. "You can come in for a moment. She's resting," the nurse said.

"Dolly, it's me, Chile Charlie," he whispered. His eyes welled, but he fought back the tears.

She opened her eyes slightly. "Chile Charlie," She smiled.

Charlie clutched her hand and kissed her forehead. He pulled up a chair next to her bed, "I'm sorry, Dolly. I never meant for you to get involved in all this." He shook his head. "And I surely didn't expect that you would get shot." His lips quivered.

Dolly was still drowsy from her surgery. "It wasn't your fault, Charlie," she said in a slow, calm voice with her eyes closed.

"I was the one who got you involved in all this. I just happened to be at the wrong place at the right time. It was an accident," Dolly said as she barely opened her eyes.

"Remember, I'm from the *projects* of North Chicago." Dolly closed her eyes and went into a deep slumber.

Nate Greystone was released from the hospital on the same evening with a mild concussion and bruises on his face. Charlie drove him back home and took the opportunity to find out what he needed to know.

"Greystone, how did you get involved in all this in the first place?"

"I wasn't involved at all. It started the day I was filling the propane tank behind the Native American Museum when Russell Strongbow came out the back door and asked me if I knew a couple of men who would do a job for him. He said it was a business deal that would pay $10,000 per person, and I would get a 'finder's fee' out of it. I knew it was going to be something terrible.

"I guess Strongbow worked at the museum, but his brown Dodge Ram was parked in the back as if he tried to hide, which I thought was weird. He returned from his truck with a small notepad and wrote down his cell number. He told me to give the note to my contact. Then he ripped off half of the notepad from the sticky part and gave it to me. He said not to use phones for communication, just the notepad."

"Was it a blue notebook? Charlie asked.

"Yeah. How did you know?" Greystone asked, surprised.

"Because I found one you wrote in Dolly's room at the El Rancho Hotel the night someone tried to rob her."

"I didn't know anything about that. I swear," Nate said apologetically. "Strongbow called me with the message. I wrote it down to give to Jimmy Running Water. That was the night before I met you and Dolly."

Charlie liked Greystone, but he would not forgive him if he had taken part in the attempted robbery at the hotel. He needed to know the extent of Greystone's involvement. "Were you with Jimmy and Chris that night?"

"No, I was gambling at Blackstone's, trying to regain my losses."

Charlie thought for a moment. That explains the whistle I heard outside that night. Chris must have been waiting somewhere in the parking lot, and Jimmy whistled to get his attention to pick him up.

"What about the Perea note?"

"I didn't write that one. Russell Strongbow called me and told me he had a note for me to give to Jimmy. I met him at the airport but couldn't find Jimmy until later. I knew nothing about Kachina masks until Jimmy and Chris accused me of stealing them. Someone took those masks, and Jimmy was mad. I hear he didn't meet with the buyer, and everybody lost half a million on the money. That's why Strongbow wanted to kill everyone."

"So, who is Li?"

"All I know is that he drives a white SUV and met with Jimmy in Tohatchi one night."

"And that information came from Strongbow when he called you, right?"

"Yeah."

Charlie felt relieved to learn Greystone was not involved directly in either crime. "You'll have to report all this to the police, you know," Charlie told him.

Chapter Eighteen

Gift of the Spirits

Detective John Trefren was sitting at his desk reading the police investigation reports when Chile Charlie walked into his office with Nate Greystone trailing behind.

"How's the investigation going, Detective?" Charlie asked.

Trefren shook his head with frustration. "Nobody's talking. So far, we have two unidentified men tying up the security guard, entering the museum, and didn't take anything. We know they were looking for something because they left a mess in the inventory room."

"You have any evidence?" Charlie asked.

"Not much. They must've been wearing gloves. All we found were a few strands of hair."

Charlie smiled at Trefren. "This is your lucky day, detective. Nate here has a story for you."

Nate told the detective about his detached involvement regarding the break-in and Jimmy, Chris, and Russell Strongbow but did not mention the masks.

"It'll be your word against theirs, and the rest is hearsay. We have no proof they were the break-in's culprits," Trefren said.

Charlie retrieved a blue notepad and the two crumbled notes from his coat pocket and placed them on Trefren's desk.

"This is the notepad that Strongbow ripped out of his notepad and gave to Nate. You'll find that the rips match the other half of the notepad in Strongbow's Dodge Ram. You can still see the imprint on the top sheet where Strongbow wrote his phone number. Nate wrote only one note, and he wrote it on the bottom sheet of the pad." Charlie pointed to one of the notes.

"This is the one written by Nate. Strongbow wrote the other one."

Trefren read and compared the two notes. "Russell Strongbow and I have been close friends since we were young. I've always known he was bad medicine," he said with sadness.

"I'm sorry to hear that," Charlie said. "If you check the phone records, you'll find that Strongbow made those phone calls to Nate, " he reported. "All the other pieces fall in place."

Nate Greystone reached into his medicine bag. "Here's your proof," he said as he placed the braided ponytail on the desk. "DNA. It was a gift from Running Water." You'll find that he was in the inventory room that night.

Detective Trefren smiled and put the evidence in a plastic bag. "I don't understand why Russell wanted to meet with Jimmy at Perea."

Charlie and Nate looked at each other, then at Trefren, and shrugged without a word.

"That leaves me with one question: who is Li?" Trefren said.

"Strongbow and Jimmy, they're the only two who know," Greystone blurted.

The room went silent.

"Three," Chile Charlie said. "I know who he is."

♦♦♦♦♦♦♦♦♦♦

Detective Trefren entered the Native American Museum with five patrol officers. He informed the female receptionist that he was there to see the museum director.

"What is this about," she asked with a frightened look.

"Tell him, private business," Trefren responded.

She entered the director's office, closed the door, and returned almost immediately.

"Mr. Acothley will see you now," she said, pointing to the door. She returned to her desk and picked up the phone.

"What can I do for you, gentleman? The director said as he stood up from his desk.

"Are you Leon Acothley, and is that your white Kia SUV parked out front," Trefren asked.

"Yes, I am, and that is my car."

Mr. Acothley had a sober look on his face. He was an older man with black rim glasses, short gray hair, and light skin, more white man than Native American. He wore western attire and an over-kill of turquoise and silver jewelry, much like Russell Strongbow—perhaps to show his link to his Navajo ancestry.

"Mr. Acothley, are you familiar with Russell Strongbow? Trefren asked.

"Why yes, the gentleman works for me."

"What exactly does he do for you?"

"He's part of the intake staff. They're responsible for obtaining and cataloging all the museum's items," Leon Acothley answered.

"Do you know a Jimmy Running Water?"

"Ah, no, no, I'm not familiar with that person," Acothley said, appearing nervous.

"Then who was that person who parked next to your KIA that night at the Tohatchi Chapter House? Trefren didn't wait for an answer. "Leon Acothley, I'm arresting you for Conspiracy of Theft of Native American artifacts."

"This must be a mistake," Acothley responded.

Detective Trefren maintained a professional police demeanor. "Sir, I have two witnesses who will testify that you were the head of the conspiracy and hired them to break into the museum to steal items for the black market."

"But nothing was taken from this museum. I didn't steal anything, and my attorney is on his way here now!" Acothley rambled in nervous confusion.

"First of all, Mr. Acothley, you're not being charged with theft, just conspiracy, and second, why did you have your receptionist call your attorney if you're innocent?"

Leon Acothley was placed into custody and escorted out of the museum by two Gallop police patrol officers.

◆◆◆◆◆◆◆◆◆◆

Detective John Trefren had arrested Jimmy Running Water and Chris Leaping Bear at Blackrock's and charged them with Attempted Robbery. The Sheriff's Department arrested Sam Blackrock for operating a gambling house, various liquor violations, using a house of prostitution, and contributing to the delinquency of minor girls. Several others were also arrested—mostly underage patrons and the ladies of the house. Several weeks later, the county condemned the house, and Blackrock's was no more.

The interrogations of the two boys went moderately well. They both claimed they went to the museum, but after searching the place, they found nothing worth taking. Chris was more cooperative and corroborated Nate's report after he was threatened with charges of kidnapping on top of burglary and attempted robbery. Chris accepted a deal, and all the charges against him were dropped, except for burglary. Jimmy Running Water was not so fortunate. On top of the other crimes, he was also charged with felony menacing and attempted murder. Neither Jimmy nor Chris ever mentioned the Kachina masks.

Chapter Nineteen

Ceremony

Two days after Dolly was released from the hospital, she and Chile Charlie drove to Magi Milly's hogan.

"So why are we going up to Milly's again?" Dolly asked.

"I don't know. Greystone called me, and he said that she wanted to tell us something important but didn't say what," Charlie explained. "Anyway, leaving that hotel room for fresh air will be good."

As they drove on the red dirt road, about a mile away from Milly's hogan, they saw several clouds of smoke rising from the direction of the house. When they neared, they saw many cars, pickup trucks, and motorcycles parked along both sides of the road leading up to the hogan.

Dolly's heartbeat increased as they got closer. "God, I hope everything is all right," she said. Maybe something happened to Milly, she thought.

There were crowds of people—men, women, children—in colorful ceremonial clothing. When they exited the car, they heard the loud pounding of drums and the chanting of songs. Behind the hogan were several bonfires and people dancing in circular directions around the fires.

Charlie took a folded wheelchair from the back of his car and helped Dolly into it. He pushed her towards the house, and then two young Navajo boys stood in front and blocked his path. One boy signaled that he would push Dolly's wheelchair.

Milly sat in her chair among a line of elderly men and women. She stood up, raised both arms and wide, holding her staff in one hand. The music and singing stopped.

"Welcome, Chile Charlie and Dolly," Magi Milly said. "These are reverent men and women. They are the Shaman, the Singers, and the Medicine people from the many tribes that make up our nation. They, and all these people, have come from distant places to honor you today."

Charlie didn't know what to say. There were so many people there. "Honor me for what," he asked.

"Chile Charlie, you have saved an ancient tradition of our people. You found the sacred Kachina masks of the ancient spirits and returned them to the Navajos. These people are here to praise you and sing songs of your journey as a way of thanks," Milly said.

Dolly reached for his hand and held it tightly. She was very proud of Charlie.

Milly sat down, and the drums and chants resumed. The people sang in perfect harmony in their colorful attire, jewelry, and feathered headbands.

"Come, Charlie, join us in dance and food. This is your day," Greystone said. He directed Charlie to a semi-circle of men sitting on the grassy ground—they looked more like warriors. Chile Charlie sat on the ground with his legs crossed, and Greystone sat beside him. Charlie noticed that Detective John Trefren sat among the semicircle of warriors.

Dolly was ushered to the other side of the ceremonial circle. A ceremonial headband was placed on her head, and women lined up on each side of her wheelchair and danced in place.

Large wool blankets were placed in front of Charlie by elderly women. A young girl approached Charlie and placed a feathered headband on his head like the other men wore. People began to enter the semi-circle with gifts for their honored guests. An older woman placed a wool blanket on Charlie's back and draped it around his shoulders. Greystone rose and approached Milly.

The music stopped again. Charlie couldn't make out what they were doing. Greystone turned and returned to the warriors' circle, and Milly followed. The music started, but this time with a slower beat of the drums and a somber chant.

Greystone enters the semi-circle with his palms up, carrying something wrapped in a red cloth. He approached Charlie with slow ceremonial movements. "Chile Charlie, it is a gift from Magi Milly and me." He unwrapped the cloth and extended his arms to Charlie. It was his Greystone's Bowie Knife.

"Greystone, that's your knife. Your grandfather gave it to you. It's been in your family for generations," Charlie told him. "I can't accept that. This should stay in your family."

"It is in the family," Milly said. "You are family now. Take it with you so you will always remember the way of the Navajo."

Charlie's throat tightened, and his eyes began to well. Dolly was not as strong as Charlie's. Her tears ran unabated.

By late afternoon, the blankets were covered with gifts made by the people: blankets, jewelry, dreamcatchers, Kachina dolls, wood carvings, and one horse saddle.

Trefren stood before Charlie and squatted in front of him. "Tell me, Charlie, how did you figure out Leon Acothley was behind the break-in?"

"That's easy. Strongbow worked at the museum and parked his car behind the building as if he were hiding. He didn't strike me as one who categorizes valuable artifacts. Who else would allow Strongbow to go in and out of the museum as if he owned the place? Director *Lee*-on Acoth-*lee*," *h*e said, pronouncing each syllable slowly with an emphasis on *Lee*.

"Charlie, you have the investigator spirit in you. By the way, this whole thing about ancient Kachina masks is just a myth, okay?" Trefren said as he nodded.

"You don't believe in them?" Charlie asked, surprised.

Trefren chuckled. "What do you think, Mr. Investigator? I'm Navajo."

◆◆◆◆◆◆◆◆◆◆

The sun began to set, and Charlie watched as Milly stood at the edge of a shallow cliff behind the hogan. Like sunrises, she loved to watch the sunsets as well. Charlie walked up and stood next to her.

"Look at the color of the desert," Milly said. "See how it changes?" She paused. "In your journey, what did you learn, Chile Charlie?"

"I learned that the spirit of my dead wife and my family will always be with me. Bodies come and go, but the spirits will always be with us."

"As with the spirit of the earth," Milly said.

Charlie's investigative curiosity overwhelmed him. He had to ask. "Milly, what happened to the Kachina masks? The day I came to see you, I left the black sack in your hogan when you went to the stables."

"The masks have returned to the desert where the Kachina spirits left them. The desert keeps its secrets and will only reveal them when ready. Mother Earth provided you with drink, food, and shelter. The desert sent the coyote and eagle spirits to direct you to the sacred masks to take and protect them. You are a good man, and the Spirits will always watch over you, Chile Charlie."

Charlie smiled and cast his eyes toward the colorful sunset. It was Milly. She had just returned from the desert when she shot Russell Strongbow. The medicine woman, Magi Milly, set out on horseback on an early winter day, returned the sacred Kachina masks to the desert, and hid them in a secret place like that body — never to be found.

THE END

Author's Notes
I cannot tell how the truth may be;
I say the tale as 'twas said to me.
Sir Walter Scott

Readers who enjoy learning about mysteries' interworking behind this author's style will find my bibliography on my website, www.georgepintarbooks.com.

My other stories featuring Chile Charlie can be purchased on Amazon.com.

Here is how you can reach me:

George Pintar

853Chile Court

Las Cruces, NM 88001

575-680-6515

Thank you in advance for sharing your interest in my work.

Made in the USA
Monee, IL
13 April 2025

15627970R00095